Memento Mori

13 Tales of Horror

Kayla Frederick

This is a work of fiction. All of the characters and events portrayed in this novel are either products of the author's imagination or are used fictitiously.

Memento Mori

Copyright © 2025 Kayla Frederick
All rights reserved.
Printed in the United States

"A Concert to Die For" was previously published in "If I Die Before I Wake Vol. 1"
"I.O.U." was previously published in "If I Die Before I Wake Vol. 2"
"When it Comes" was previously published in "Just a Girl"
"Dolls" & "Mirror Image" were previously published in "Flirting with Death: A Collection of Short Stories & Poems"
"Don't Look", "Fear", "Happy Birthday", & "Stockholm Syndrome" were previously published in "When Night Falls"

No part of this book may be reproduced in any form, including photocopying, recording, or other electronic or mechanical methods—except in the case of brief quotations embodied in articles or reviews—without written permission by the publisher.

Cover by betibup33
Edited by Markedup Editing

ISBN: 978-1-950530-44-1
Library of Congress Control Number: 2024912827
First Edition March 2025

https://authorkaylafrederick.com

Other Books by Kayla Frederick

The Residency
What I Did
After the Devil
Flirting with Death
Voices

Table of Contents

1. I.O.U. — pg. 1-24

2. A Concert to Die For — pg. 27-56

3. When it Comes — pg. 59-86

4. Dolls — pg. 89-106

5. Footsteps — pg. 109-140

6. The Day You Killed Me — pg. 143-168

7. Secrets of the Quiet Visitor — pg. 171-190

8. Don't Look — pg. 193-200

9. Stockholm Syndrome — pg. 203-218

10. Dreamcatcher — pg. 221-230

11. Mirror Image — pg. 233-252

12. Fear — pg. 255-264

13. Happy Birthday — pg. 267-278

Never stick your nose where it doesn't belong—it might get chopped off.

I.O.U.

1.

THE SCRAPE OF the landscaping bag moving over the grass was soothing to Mason, the whispery sound like a nightmarish lullaby. Inside the bag, there were no yard trimmings or twigs. It contained his sixth victim. As he moved, he thought back through the night from the first moment he'd spotted her at the bar to the second the light had disappeared from her brown eyes. He pictured her face, her expression before he grabbed her. Usually, he didn't like to risk his captures in the middle of the city. There were witnesses and cameras, but this girl had so perfectly matched his ideal type—long brown hair and a pretty face.

He didn't know what it was about brown hair that stirred him up. Maybe it had something to do with the sister he'd had a falling out with a decade before, or maybe it was because of his mother. Who could say?

With this girl, all he'd wanted to do was brush her hair over and over until it fluffed up. Of course that had been *before* he took her scalp off, keeping the beautiful locks as a trophy along with the other five he'd gathered.

The summer night made the job of digging a pit harder, his pudgy hands sweating more than usual, making the handle of the shovel slippery. He cursed every time he lost his hold and the old handle presented him with a new splinter. So badly, he wanted to buy a new shovel, but he feared it would be used to track him for his crimes.

An owl hooted in the distance, and Mason paused long enough to wipe the sweat from his forehead with a handkerchief. He was getting older, that much was obvious. He didn't have the stamina that he once had and every victim took more time to dispose of than the one before. It wouldn't be much longer before he wouldn't be able to do it anymore. When the pit was big enough, he glanced over to the garbage bag beside him. With an exaggerated groan, he pulled himself out of the hole, kicked the body inside, and started to cover it with dirt.

He was tired and achy, his adrenaline dropping rapidly, and the fear that he was going to be seen, was rising. Sweat covered him in an unpleasant sheen. He longed for a shower and sleep and wanted to get away from his crime as quickly as possible. While that had been true of all his victims, it was especially pertinent in this case. This one had given him the worst scare of his life. His heart still pounded at the sound of her piercing scream bouncing around the city street, and the distinct sound of a man shouting *"Hey"* from the distance.

Whoever the man had been, he'd been close enough to see Mason grab the girl which meant he could see *him*. He could give details to the police, details could lead to a police sketch, which could lead to an arrest. Mason could've shrugged it all off. His appearance didn't particularly stand out. A receding hairline, bulging stomach, and height that let him blend in the crowd. But the fact his license plate could've been read *did* worry him.

What if the man had taken a picture?

MEMENTO MORI

What if, what if, what if… the questions swirled inside his mind like a mantra he didn't want to adopt. He could torture himself for days with his own anxiety.

Pushing it away was a battle he would not win, so he tried to think one step ahead. Once the plastic was covered and the dirt evened out, Mason made it out of the woods and back to his truck. The drive home was a bit more serene, though he kept his eyes on the rearview mirror, paranoid a cop would appear at any minute, see his plates, and pull him over.

When he got home, he drove his truck into the backyard and got out. He rummaged through the toolbox he kept in the bed, getting a screwdriver to pry the damning plate off. Wrapping it up in some plastic sheets from his trunk, he tossed it into his trash can with a *thump*. With any luck, it would be transported away to the dump with no one being any the wiser to where it had come from. He screwed a new plate on his truck from the pile he always kept on hand. From his first kill onward, he'd been wary of something like tonight happening, so he'd had the foresight to buy several.

Now he was glad.

It wasn't much in the way of peace of mind, but it would lay the foundation for it. He let his tired feet lead the way inside and directly to the kitchen, desperate to drown himself in alcohol. He had a shelf dedicated to his habit, covered in bottles of varying volume. Mason selected his half empty bottle of scotch, tipping it down his throat greedily as he settled on the couch.

He was on the brink of dozing off when a scream echoed through his mind, the wail from the woman earlier, and he was jolted out of the state of semi-sleep, heart hammering in his chest.

KAYLA FREDERICK

When his surroundings came into focus, he relaxed a bit.

He was at home. He was safe.

How true would that be the next time I go hunting?

He pulled the scalp from his pocket. The blood had dried, and it was starting to emit a smell, but the hair was still soft. He lifted it to his nose, but the sweet scent of the woman was gone. Disappointed, he tossed it onto the cushion next to him.

I'll never smell that scent again.

An idea came to him, a new way to reel in victims that might be a little less risky than casing out a place and picking one up off the street. The internet offered all sorts of new opportunities for people of every lifestyle. What if he placed an ad? People had all sorts of fetishes, maybe someone out there had a fantasy about being murdered.

Crazier things had happened, right?

It can be tracked, he reminded himself, the hope dying as quickly as it had blossomed.

Maybe on the normal internet that was the case, but the Dark Web was a place where chaos roamed free. Police scoped it out all the time but the odds of them being able to trace anything, especially his digital footsteps, were slim to none. Thousands of people get away with things on the Dark Web every day. Mason himself had done some things he wasn't particularly proud of with people he had met there.

In his drunken stupor, he was overjoyed with his idea. He stood up, his massive frame wobbling, before he crossed the house, scooping up his laptop from where he'd left it on the table beside his bed. He carried it into his work room, setting it down on the desk before he settled himself into the chair. The wooden

MEMENTO MORI

frame creaked under his weight as he set up Tor to navigate to the Dark Web.

Maybe this was an idiotic idea, but if anyone knew the odds of him pulling this off successfully, it would be these people. They might have tips, be able to point him in the right direction of breaking the law. After all, a few of them operated legal red rooms and got away with it all because of the way they worded their contracts. And yes, they had *contracts*. Hiding in plain sight? It was a beautiful concept. One he was surprised he hadn't tried to exploit sooner.

Mason began to type. English had never been his best subject, but he knew what he wanted, and that was what fueled him to push through all the nagging worries. He paused, tapping a chubby finger on the wooden desk. A huge appeal of the victims he chose was their innocence. Would he really be able to find that in anyone browsing through the Dark Web?

It's worth a try, he told himself as he pulled up the website.

He didn't know of a website where serial killers could post what they were after, but he did know of one that was similar to what he needed, a sex trafficking ring, known for kidnapping people requested by users. He'd write his post directed at his potential audience instead.

For the sake of anonymity, I'm not going to post my name. I will go by the name of X. I am seeking out the perfect person to fulfill a certain urge of mine. In order to apply, this person must fit the following criteria:

~Be female between the ages of 20 and 25

~Brown hair preferred but not required

~Must be a willing participant who will not try to escape

KAYLA FREDERICK

If you meet these criteria, and don't mind the fact that you will not be walking away from the encounter, you are encouraged to seek me out. If it sweetens the deal at all, I can arrange a payment to next of kin to at least cover funeral expenses.

~X

At the bottom, he added an encrypted email link where anyone reading the ad could message him. He did his best to ensure it couldn't be tracked back to him. The last thing he wanted was for someone on the Dark Web to hack it and get his information. There was no telling what they'd do with it.

The cursor hovered over the post button as Mason reread his work. Satisfied, he sat back, clicked on it, and watched as the screen loaded. In a weird way, he was proud of himself. He had never been a sharp thinker, but as far as he could tell, this was a good idea.

Would that still be the case when morning—and sobriety—came? There was no way to know until tomorrow. He stood up, vision spotted with black circles before he sat back down, passing out onto his desk.

MEMENTO MORI

2.

WHEN MASON WOKE up, the first thing he did was groan from the immense pain building up in the front of his skull and the back of his neck. He sat up, and his stomach sloshed with a similar protest, and he froze, wondering if he would puke up everything in his stomach. Hangovers hadn't bothered him in his twenties. When he hit thirty, they started to get rougher, but now that he was in his forties, they were nearly fatal. He told himself that at any time he could stop subjecting himself to this anguish, but the only cure was more alcohol.

It was a vicious cycle.

He'd fallen asleep on his computer, the keyboard leaving marks on his face. The sick feeling in his gut worsened as reality crept through the migraine, reminding him about everything he had tried to repress. The memories came first as flashes of Six's face then it was followed by the close call with the man and his idea about the dark web.

He tapped his laptop to bring it back to life. His ad stared at him from the black background. "What was I thinking?" he asked out loud.

The writing was coherent enough, but it was a ridiculous plan. The last thing he needed to do was call attention to himself. He tried to maneuver to the settings, desperate to delete it. It would get no responses, he was sure. After all, no one *wants* to be murdered.

Drunk me is dumber than sober me, he lamented.

If anyone responded, it would most likely be the

kidnappers on the site offering their assistance or their anger at him for clogging up their feed. In the daylight, the stupidity of his drunken brain was enough to make him laugh so hard, his stomach started to protest again. Serial killers were supposed to be smart, weren't they?

"Ugh," he groaned, wiping his hand down his face as the screen loaded.

The ad wasn't there. After refreshing to double check that it was really gone, he maneuvered to the encrypted email he'd attached to it, not expecting anything to be in it. A glowing *one* flashed in the corner. He had a message. Mason didn't want to open it, worried it would be a hacker trying to send him malware.

Delete it. Don't read it.

After all, the beast within him would be quenched for at least a week or so before the urge to kill would come back. All of this was superfluous.

But this could be a willing victim, he thought as the cursor hovered over the button.

He hated that urge, the greedy unquenchable need to kill. It was a beast he couldn't satisfy. Puffing his cheeks, he clicked on it with one ill-timed press of the button and the message was before him.

X,

It's nice to meet you, I think. I read your ad, and I am interested in the service you are providing. I'm twenty years old so I fit your description. I haven't seen the upside of life for a while. Dying doesn't frighten me. I'd be perfectly happy with being your next victim, and I won't require any monetary

MEMENTO MORI

gain either. Let me know the time and place to meet you, and I'll be there.

—Y

Mason was elated on the first read, but during the reread, the suspicion began to sink in. What kind of person would willingly walk to their death without trying to get money out of it for the ones they were leaving behind?

Mason scoffed. *This has to be the police. This is like one of those 20/20 busts.*

He was uneasy again and wished he would've never had this idea. It seemed all he had done was put himself directly on the police's radar and if not the police's then *someone's*.

He deleted the email.

Forcing himself to stand up, he went to the kitchen and made breakfast. The smell of cooking eggs had his stomach sloshing all over again, but he tried to tell himself that food would help. That something other than staring at the screen with his failures would do him good.

It made no difference. Y was at the front of his mind the entire time. Y. Considering she could've put anything, it was an interesting choice for a signature.

That's what they want you to think, he scolded himself.

He made a plate and sat down at the table. The scent flooded his nostrils, making his mouth water with a sickening mix of hunger and nausea. He dropped the fork with a clatter. He wouldn't be able to eat it. Gritting his teeth, he gave up on breakfast, dumping the entirety of his food into the trash before tossing his plate in the sink. He went to the bathroom, puked, and got himself ready for work, feeling better with some of the alcohol out of his system.

    A glance at the mirror told him he didn't look it, though, but it didn't matter. His job at the local butcher shop only required that he show up. Mason avoided the computer as he passed back through the living room and went out to his truck. All he wanted to do was forget about last night, but the drive to work had him wracked with fear that his fake plates would be called out for being such.

    They weren't, and he made it without incident. Thanks to his appearance, people assumed he was unfriendly, unsocial, and so he was left alone at work. With the headache still throbbing at his temples, he was grateful. By the time the end of his shift came, he was barely able to keep his eyes open.

    His boss dismissed him, and Mason was once again faced with a nerve-wracking ride in his truck. Back home, he stepped into the living room, and his eyes went instantly to his computer. As he stripped off his shoes and coat, he tried to tell himself to go past it, to go to bed, but his curiosity was piqued at the morning's message. She was all he could think about. Groaning, he plopped down at his desk and opened his email. The blinking icon indicated a brand-new message.

    X,

I don't mean to pry if you've already found someone, but this isn't the police if that's what you're thinking. I'm in no way affiliated with them or anyone really. I'm ready to go and too much of a coward to do it myself. Please consider responding. I'm patient. I'll wait for whenever you're ready.

MEMENTO MORI

—Y

Mason hadn't realized he'd broken into a smile until he finished reading. He'd spent all day trying to tell himself that the perfect girl didn't exist, that this was a trap, but this email felt real. Some part of his intuition said he could trust her because he could recognize the desperation seeping through the computer. There were times he'd felt like this. Times when he wanted the world to ease up.

Bad idea or not, he hit reply.

KAYLA FREDERICK

3.

ON A NORMAL hunt, Mason always considered the cleanup and disposal part of his process to be the most difficult step. On this one? The grabbing was going to be tough, and that was ironic since the entire point of this idea had been to make it easier. Getting ready to go out, his heart skipped wildly, torn between the desire for this to truly be happening and the fear that it was all a set up and he was about to get himself sent to jail for the rest of his life.

Y had given a description of herself—thin, with long brown hair, blue eyes, and a slight limp to her walk from an accident in her teenage years. To him, she sounded exactly like the other girls he'd mangled, and that only further fueled his belief that this was the police. They kept track of things like that, similarities in victims, and based on his ad, it would be too easy to assume who the poster was.

It was too late to back out now, and he didn't want to. Whoever Y was, he wanted to meet her, wanted to see what twenty-year-old would willingly throw her life away. Fearing giving out his address would lead to a raid, he gave her the address of the abandoned house at the corner of the street. It was close to his house, which he knew police would also take into consideration, but he didn't want to go out far. The farther he had to travel with her in tow, the higher the chances were that he would be seen. And that didn't need to happen again. He gave her the instructions to show up alone at midnight. She would go inside the house and wait for him there.

MEMENTO MORI

A half hour away from midnight, readiness prickled his skin. He wanted to be out the door, to be there when she arrived, but he had to remind himself that wasn't a good idea. If he wanted to get away with this, he needed to be smart about it, to study every detail because it might be important later on. So, he bided his time. About ten minutes before midnight, he slipped out his backdoor, pulling his hood up as he traveled down the sidewalk.

The lights in the neighbors' houses were all dark. The only benefit of living in a neighborhood of older residents, was the fact that they all had early bedtimes. It made it easier for him to travel unnoticed, on his own street at least. As he approached the lot with the house, he ducked into the shadows of the nearby yard, scanning every place he could see from his hiding place.

Midnight arrived, and every part of him wanted to leap into action, but he had to quell the instinct until his surveillance was done. There were no cars in the street that he didn't recognize. Two were visible from the building but both of them belonged to his neighbors. Mason glanced toward the building, the empty lot of land around it adding to its creepy aesthetic. He hadn't seen Y appear yet and wondered if she was going to back out. He moved along the bushes, scanning for anything out of place.

"Huh," he said when he found nothing.

Something moved near the street. A woman appeared from the shadows, the darkness a shocking contrast to the paleness of her skin. Her waist length golden brown hair swung with her every step, more visible against her bright red coat, and Mason's jaw dropped open. By far, she was the most beautiful of any of the others, and he wondered if there was some kind of mistake. Surely a woman like *this* wouldn't want to die?

She scanned her surroundings, and he wondered what she was looking for. A second later, she crossed the lot, the dilapidated old building in the distance not daunting to her at all, it seemed. She stepped up onto the tiny stone porch and pulled the door open. From where Mason crouched, he could see the darkness inside, but it didn't slow her down. She stepped through it, letting the door close behind her. Mason's heart started to pound with the familiar thrill of the hunt. His favorite part was watching his victim when they didn't know he was there. Now that he had actually *seen* her, he wanted this so much more.

It was getting harder to focus. He breathed through the excitement, doing another scope for any watching eyes. There were still none. As far as he could tell, she'd come alone, as he had instructed. On instinct, he stuck to the shadows as he approached the building, contemplating what kind of an entrance he wanted to make.

This is stupid.

What did it matter? He never spent so much time thinking about first impressions when he grabbed his victims off the street. It wasn't something that factored in, so Y should be no different. Steeling himself, he barged inside, unsure of what he would see. She sat in the middle of the room Indian-style, the light from a nearby window trickling over her. Her eyes were closed, her hands resting on her knees, and he had to hold back his surprise. He didn't know what he had expected her to be doing, but it certainly wasn't *meditating.*

The door slammed behind him, and her eyes opened. In the dark, he couldn't tell what color they were, but they were large, exaggerated by the shadows, and he noted how small the rest of her face was in comparison. In a way, she reminded him of an anime character, and he didn't know what to do with that information.

"X?" she asked in a soft, musical voice.

Mason resisted the urge to mutter out something stupid and replied with a similar question. "Y?"

She climbed to her feet. "Okay, so how does this work? What's your process?"

Mason drew his eyebrows together as he stared at her. How could someone be so *upbeat* about their own demise? It made his skin crawl. Her plump lips curved into a smile as she waited for his response. She actually wanted to *know* what he was going to do to her, but he didn't want to explain it. For some reason, that made it perverse, *wrong*, and he didn't want anything to make him mess up this kill. She was his perfect victim after all.

"Am I asking too many questions?" she asked after the silence extended into a full minute.

"Just come with me," he said in a gruff voice two octaves lower than his usual tone. His uncertainties were dangerously close to coming out, and he wanted to hide them deep down where they would never see the light of day.

"Okay," she said, allowing him to lead the way out of the building.

Despite her limp, she was able to keep up with him. He cut her a sideways glance and frowned. He'd wanted to intimidate her, to stop her from smiling, but her demeanor didn't change. There wasn't exactly a *happy* expression on her face, but the slightly upturned corners of her lips ensured it was still positive in nature.

He couldn't understand it.

Wary of any witnesses, he pulled the hood up more around his face. Y made no such gesture. He looked at her from the corner of his eye again, thinking how distinctive her hair was.

So many risks.

Again, he let out a little prayer of gratitude that his elderly neighbors were asleep. Y was the kind of girl they would've asked him questions about later. Once they were inside his house, and the door closed behind them, Mason wasn't sure how to proceed. Y stood toe to toe with him, waiting expectantly for what he'd promised, but it was awkward now.

With the other girls, this was the part where he dragged them to the basement, the sounds of their terror ramping up the monster inside him. The predator was piqued of course, but it was more with morbid curiosity than the desire to fill a need.

He looked into Y's eyes for a fraction of a second but had to pull his gaze away. There was electricity when he stared into them, as if he could feel the soul he was about to steal. Desperate to stir up the beast inside of him, he grabbed her wrist, harder than necessary, but she didn't protest. Her arm went slack, and she came with him as he led the way down the stairs.

When they reached the bottom, he flicked on the light, illuminating his own personal Red Room. There was a silver table in the middle of the room, brown patches still spilled across it from Six. He'd been so swept up in his fear and idea for his next victim that he hadn't taken the time to properly clean up. The myriad of tools on the tiny tray beside the table were in the same state.

MEMENTO MORI

I'm getting sloppy. That sent a shock of fear down his spine. If he could've forgotten about something as important as cleaning up, what else had he forgotten?

He expected some sort of reaction, but Y had none. Her huge eyes swept over every inch of the room. "You should really invest in some plastic wrap," she said and turned away toward the table. "Clothes on or off?"

Before he could respond, she started stripping the layers to the floor. Her coat went first followed by the white dress she wore underneath. Pale skin exposed, she took her place on the table, not flinching when the congealed blood smeared onto her arms.

Mason stared at her. For everything he'd ever seen in his life, this was perhaps the strangest moment he had ever encountered. He couldn't help his eyes from running from her head, down to her feet, and back again. Without fear, the basement was silent, and he wasn't used to that. There was no fear in her eyes, and he wasn't used to that either. He stared at the straps hanging limply at the sides of the table.

He didn't need them today.

"Whenever you're ready," Y said and moved her eyes back to the ceiling.

Mason started to wonder if he was still drunk and all of this was some sort of dream that he couldn't wake up from. It was too perfect and too wrong all at the same time. In a daze, he moved to the tray, picking up a bloody scalpel before he turned toward the table. He tried to swing but couldn't bring himself to do it.

"Why?" he demanded, swinging his hand so hard that the

scalpel pinged off the edge of the table.

"Huh?"

"Why are you here, so *ready* for your death?" he asked. "How are you not scared? I'm so used to listening to people pleading for their lives and this is…is…"

Y jutted her bottom lip out into a pout. "Do you want me to beg? Will that make it better for you?"

Mason flared his nostrils, angry for a reason he couldn't understand. "No. I just can't imagine what would drive someone like you to make this decision."

"I didn't think it mattered *why* I was here, I thought it just mattered that I *was* here," Y countered. "I could ask you plenty of questions too, you know? I could demand to know what makes a person like you want to do this to someone else. I could ask you why you like girls with brown hair. I could ask you how many others you've killed. But I won't because it's simply not my place."

Mason pursed his lips. She was right. Her presence didn't mean she owed him an explanation. The deal was that she'd show up, and she'd done that. Now he had to fulfill his end of the agreement.

MEMENTO MORI

4.

MASON WOULDN'T ADMIT out loud how hard it was for him to lower the scalpel to her stomach, but when he did, he smiled with pleasure at the first slice. Part of him had been so convinced that she wouldn't react to this either after how emotionless she had been so far, but as soon as the metal sunk into her skin, she screamed.

The familiar sound echoed off the walls and mixed with the metallic odor of her blood, and his smile grew. The monster inside of him was beginning to feel right at home. Gash after gash, he freed blood from the girl, and she started to quiet.

He paused, studying her.

"Don't...stop," she wheezed.

Her skin, which had started off a shade of porcelain tinted pinkish with life, was now ghost-like. Mason paused to watch as the first drop of blood slipped from the table to join the muck already gathered on the floor. The devastation was bad, but her chest continued to rise and fall, and he couldn't contain his surprise. The fact she had survived *this* long was nothing short of a miracle. She'd made it far longer than any of the other victims, and he didn't want this moment to end. He felt powerful, in control, and almost considered keeping the girl alive to extend this feeling to another day.

The blood made the scalpel slippery, and he stepped away to wipe it off before approaching her again. If he could feel anything close to human emotions, this would be what happiness was like. He hoped she could *feel* his gratitude for giving him this opportunity. By the time he went to lower the scalpel again, she took a massive breath, and her head lolled to the side.

Mason lowered the scalpel to his side before he tossed it onto the tray. His eyes ran over his work, and he gave her a tiny nod before searching for his ream of trash bags on the other side of the room, pondering leaving her on the table overnight. He felt safe in his assumption that since she'd come willingly, no one would be searching for her. Or at least he hoped she'd taken the time to make the arrangements so they wouldn't.

A gasp of breath made him whisk around. Y moved her head, her chest rising and falling with shallow breaths. Drawing his eyebrows together, Mason picked up the scalpel again, approaching her with an eyebrow raised.

"You were dead," he said.

A rugged gasp tore through Y's chest, but she said nothing.

Mason breathed out, cutting a line along the bottom of her ribs. The new cut didn't bleed like the others had, and he tried to push it in deeper until the metal scraped against bone with an unpleasantly shrill noise. Y made no reaction, and he lifted the scalpel. Before his eyes, the wound started to heal, the red fading at the corners, before it closed to a slit and disappeared. One by one, the rest of her wounds did the same, leaving perfect porcelain skin behind.

Mason was angry. *Frustrated.* How could this be happening? What *was* this girl? In a fit of fury, he slashed again and again and again, meeting the same result every time. At last, his energy started to dwindle, and he had to stop to take a break. As he watched, every wound healed completely. It was as if someone had pressed rewind on their session, taking them back to the moment Y had lain down on the table.

"I don't understand," he said, gasping to catch his breath, unsure if he were talking to her or himself.

She sat up, legs swishing over the edge of the table, smeared with a mix of fresh and congealed blood. After giving herself a quick pat down, she looked up at him. "I appreciate you trying."

Mason's mind was blown beyond the point of coming up with a coherent response. "What?"

"This? I was hoping it would work. You seemed like a sure-fire thing, but I guess this wasn't the answer I needed," she said and hopped off the table. She didn't slide in the blood and her feet made no sound as she bent over to scoop up her clothes.

"What answer?" Mason asked, tipping his head to try and catch her eye. Without it, he felt as if she were dismissing him, pushing him away.

"Oh, my. You look so confused," she said and pulled her dress on. She put her coat overtop, her long brown hair sleek and shiny as she tossed it over her shoulder. He stared at it, yearning to give it a hard yank to feel as if he were back in control of the situation. After straightening out her coat, she said, "Don't feel bad, okay? Here's the deal, I'm already dead."

"You're ... *dead?*" Mason asked, feeling as if he had lost all ability to create his own words. All he could do was echo her.

She bobbed her head. "Mmhmm. I was murdered *years* ago. They never figured out who did it, and I've been stuck here ever since. Not too long after it all happened, I ran into someone, a man. He told me the gist of my situation, told me that I was here for a reason, and if I wanted to move on, I needed to deal with what had happened to me. Now, I've heard about ghosts being stuck because of a tragedy, and I figured my case wasn't going to be solved anytime soon, so I believed that if I solved it, I could move on. Guess not."

"You replied to my ad," he stated, stupidly.

"Yes."

"How? If you're dead, how could you do that? How could you *bleed*?"

"Something to think about, isn't it?" she asked and thrust her hands into her pockets. "Truth is, the man never really told me *why* I was like this, and I figured it had something to do with my mission. I went through a period where I thought if I avenged myself, if I put down the men who did this, then it would free me. I killed two men, but I'm still here. That means that I was either wrong in my choice or that there were others involved."

Mason stared into her eyes. The longer he did, the more familiar she looked, and he tried to keep the fear off his face. It had been a long time since One had died, so long ago that he wasn't sure exactly how it had happened. It had been an accident, a drunken hit and run that had resulted in him burying a body in the middle of the night before anyone could realize what he'd done.

"Thanks for your time. It was nice meeting you," Y said and stepped delicately through the mess to peck him on the cheek.

She made a move for the door when Mason's voice stopped her. "When did you say you died?"

"Oh, I don't know. A few years ago?" she said and tipped her head. "Why do you ask?"

MEMENTO MORI

A few years ago, he thought, mind flashing through the images of the drive through the dark, the thump of a body, the long brown hair matted with blood.

Her piercing eyes searched his face, catching every change in emotion as she crept toward him. Mason was so lost in his memories that he didn't notice when she slid the scalpel from his fingers. When he finally made eye contact, she stabbed the blade into the side of his neck. Pain flooded through him, and he reached up, blood pooling around his fingers as he collapsed to his knees.

Y took a step backward as he choked and gasped for air. "*You* were the one," she whispered, voice an ethereal growl instead of the lilting tone she'd used so far.

"I-I'm sorry," he choked out. "I-It was…an acci-dent."

Y closed her eyes before she dropped to her knees beside him. Her eyes didn't leave his as she pulled out the scalpel and stabbed him directly through the heart. Mason's peripheral vision darkened as the life seeped out of him. Before his vision cut to black, he was offered an image of Y and a man with a black hood before consciousness left him forever.

KAYLA FREDERICK

MEMENTO MORI

With the good must come the bad. For every wish? A curse.

KAYLA FREDERICK

MEMENTO MORI

A Concert to Die For

1.

ISAAC STARED AT the pennies in the bottom of his guitar case. It wasn't much money, possibly a little over a dollar altogether. This was probably the worst night he had ever endured. It certainly wasn't worth the hours he'd already spent playing. He bent down to pick up each individual coin, but one of the pennies stuck to the lining in his case. Gum. Someone had thrown gum. Frustrated, he tossed the change back into the case and carefully set his instrument on top. The guitar, a black and gold Yamaha acoustic guitar he'd been given on his fifteenth birthday, was perhaps his most prized possession.

He picked up the tiny bottle of tequila he'd bought on his way to the station and swigged the last sip. As hard as he could, Isaac tossed the bottle into the nearest trashcan, enjoying the sound of broken glass. He tried to not let his emotions show after that, as he lugged his guitar away, but inside, he was in turmoil.

For as long as he could remember, it had been his dream to play the guitar professionally. He'd learned to play when he was twelve after bugging his mother for lessons and hoped to craft his life around the skill. But almost a decade later, he spent his evenings in the subway, earning less and less.

Yet never before had a night gone so *badly*.

This was not the future he'd envisioned for himself. Isaac

boarded the subway and sat down, setting the guitar next to him before he buried his face in his hands. He couldn't wait to make it home. The world felt too bright, too crowded. He didn't want to admit that playing the guitar was getting him nowhere, that the time he put in could be better used going to college and making friends.

A long time ago, he had told himself that if life wasn't what he wanted by twenty-five, that he would give into his parent's wishes, and go to college and get a real job. His birthday was a week away. If he had to give up on his dream, what was the point of life?

Desperation pushed him to keep trying. For the past month, he spent every moment that he wasn't at work, playing guitar in random places across town. The great thing about America was that anyone could achieve their dreams with hard work, determination, and luck, right?

But it was getting harder to ignore his doubts. At the very least, he should've had *some* job related to the music industry. Instead, he was a dishwasher and partly worried he always would be. That thought doubled with the tequila had him on the verge of tears.

Don't cry, he told himself, biting into his lip until the metallic tang of blood flooded his senses.

A sob or two still made its way free. He expected to see everyone's eyes on him, but they weren't. Weird things happened on the subway every day, so the regulars had learned the meaning of minding their own business. Isaac felt a bit better coming to that realization. He wiped his eyes and tried to play it off, except one man *was* staring at him.

MEMENTO MORI

A green hat shadowed his eyes, but Isaac could make out a sharp face beneath the brim. The man's brown coat came up high around his shoulders, hiding a portion of his neck. No one sat in the seat beside him, and Isaac scoffed, guessing why. He looked like just another New York wino.

Isaac ignored him, getting ready to get off the subway. When his stop came, he charged through everyone, paying no attention to the angered cries, and hurried up the stairs into the darkness. He pulled another tiny bottle of liquor from his pocket, downing it in one sip. The shatter of glass when the bottle hit the pavement was more satisfying than the first had been.

His vision swirled, and he stumbled over his feet, letting the warmth of the alcohol soothe away all his pain. A block away from his apartment, a sense of dizziness overcame him. He bent to hurl into the bushes, wincing at the burning in his abdomen. He tried to keep walking, but the pain intensified, and he set the guitar case down, tucking his head between his knees, preparing himself to puke again. Breathing in and out to try to clear the sensation of water moving in his head, he started to sweat and right before the sickening feeling dissolved, he heard footsteps.

Glancing over his shoulder, he saw nobody in the shadows. *I really gotta stop drinking,* he thought and forced himself to his feet. He grabbed the case, the clinking of coins not causing him the despair it had earlier. *Tomorrow is a new day.*

With the feeling of being watched, by real people or imaginary demons, he couldn't tell, but he didn't want to stick around to find out. He walked a little farther when the sound of footsteps came again. Glancing over his shoulder caused him to trip over the curb before him. Caught off guard, he struggled to keep his balance, and the guitar case popped open, sending his precious instrument careening onto the pavement with an unpleasant *crack*.

"No, no, no!" he whimpered and hurried over to it on his hands and knees. He picked it up, staring at the dents and tiny crack in the bottom of the frame. "Fuck!" he yelled, not caring who heard him. Desperately, he tried to push the pieces back into place, but the crack only deepened.

Thick tears flooded down his cheeks as he stared at his broken guitar. He couldn't afford to buy a new one, and there was no telling how much it would cost to repair this. He plucked a string, listening to the off-key *thwack*.

"What happened here?" a sickeningly sweet voice poured from the shadows.

Isaac gasped. It was the man from the subway. The one with the green hat and brown coat. He loomed a few feet away. Without the lights from the train, his face was consumed by the darkness except for the tiny gleam of his eyes.

"The fuck's it look like?" Isaac snapped, angrily rapping the back of his hand against the strings. "I broke my guitar."

"That's unfortunate."

"What's it to you?" Isaac snarled. He set the instrument in its case, trying to pick as many of the tiny pieces up as he could.

In the back of his head, he was aware that something wasn't right, that maybe he shouldn't turn his back on the man. Sober, he would've been fully alarmed that he'd been followed from the subway, but in the moment, his mind was stuck on the day he'd weathered and the remains of his most prized possession in his hands.

MEMENTO MORI

"I can fix it for you," the man offered as Isaac snapped the case closed.

He crouched beside him, and Isaac flinched away, not realizing how close he was until that moment. "And why would you do that?"

His breath was sharp, almost rancid as he said, "Seems a shame for anyone to give up on their dreams."

Isaac stared at him with both suspicion and hope. Part of him was sure this was a trick, that the man was setting him up to rob him, but the idea someone could possibly fix his beloved guitar was too tempting.

"What do you want in return?" Isaac asked.

"Patience, my good friend. I'll let you know when the time comes." He reached out his hand. "What do you say?"

Isaac had no second thoughts as he slid his hand into the strange man's.

2.

ISAAC WOKE WITH a gasp, black hair matted to his forehead with sweat. His entire body felt clammy, and the dark stillness of his room confused him. He couldn't remember going to bed the night before. One moment, he'd been staring at the strange man with the odd coat and hat, and the next, he was home.

He patted himself over, feeling his mouth go dry as he remembered his guitar. He hurried across the room to where his case leaned on the wall beside the door and opened it, dreading what he would see. Inside, the guitar was picture perfect. He pulled it out of the case, running his finger over bottom where it had smashed into the concrete. The shiny surface glowed back, in better shape than it'd been in years.

Isaac scratched the back of his neck, glancing around his room for answers that weren't there. *It was a dream,* he told himself. The entire evening had been a figment of his imagination. That was all. The result of too little sleep and too much alcohol.

He stood up, pushing his wet hair back from his eyes as he glanced at the clock. It was late, *he* was late. Cursing under his breath, he got dressed, wishing he could've showered because the sour stench of old alcohol clung to him, and hurried out the door. He ran most of the way, nearly bursting through the restaurant-door like a madman.

His boss looked up at him from the hostess' stand, displeasure apparent. "You're late," she said, tapping her fingers on the polished surface of a stack of menus.

"I know, I'm sorry," Isaac said, running a hand across his

face in the hopes of removing any traces of his rough night. "I lost track of time."

"This is the third time this week," she said, wrinkling her nose as she approached him. He knew she smelt alcohol. "If it happens again, I'm gonna have to let you go."

"But—"

"No excuses," she said, raising an eyebrow to glare at him before she walked off.

Isaac opened his mouth to argue but gave up. After all, what could he say? He didn't care about this job. It was a way to pay the bills. That was all. He hadn't expected to be here more than a month or two.

That had been a year ago.

The bad mood from last night began to leech its way into his bones again.

"Another late night?" the cook, Rudy, called to him as he trudged into the backroom.

Isaac gave him the stink-eye. Rudy was a good guy, but he wasn't feeling up to conversation. He wanted the day to be over. Isaac went to the bathroom, splashing water on his face. His silver eyes looked more absent than usual, and he attributed that to the pain throbbing in his skull. Resigning himself to another long shift, he went to work.

When his day was over, he took his time getting home. The longer he spent walking, the better he began to feel. He had a hankering for a drink. Different venues arranged themselves in his mind, and he considered grabbing his guitar and making the best of his options. His skin prickled when his mind took a tangent to the strange man.

He's not real, Isaac tried to tell himself.

Something in him couldn't be convinced.

There's no way he could've fixed my guitar like that, he reasoned.

When he closed his eyes, the tiny prick from the shards of his guitar stabbing into his finger could still be felt. He hadn't imagined *all* of that, right? Sweat formed on his temples when he arrived home, but he wiped it away and crouched beside his case. He popped it open and studied his instrument again, running his fingers over the spot where it had been devastated. It was smooth, as if it had never been broken.

That's because it hasn't, he told himself. That was the only answer that made sense.

When he closed his eyes, he could still see the man's face so clearly, his eerie grin in the shadows, and told himself that people were incapable of making up faces. That meant that in *some* way, he was real. He had to be. The only way to prove it would be to go back, to find him again. Apprehension filled Isaac's stomach, but there was one thing he wasn't—a quitter. Putting his beanie on over his black hair, he grabbed the black case and went out the door.

***

ISAAC DECIDED TO go to the exact same place he'd tried the night before. The night of mere pennies had hurt him down to his soul, but he was determined to see if the strange man would appear again. If last night really had happened like he remembered it, he would expect Isaac's payment.

Isaac got on the subway, eyes alert, scanning the faces of

every passenger until he got annoyed glances back.

The man wasn't among them.

Feeling slightly put out, Isaac got off at his stop and moved to his favorite corner. It was slightly off the path, so it was shadowy, but not so much so that he would blend into the background. Setting down his bag, Isaac set the guitar case open toward the stream of passing people and picked up the guitar. He took a breath, surveying the crowd and the mood before him before he began to play.

His eyes stayed on the ground, studying the folds of the black satin liner inside the case. For some reason, starting was the hardest part of a performance. It was almost awkward. Once he was in the moment, and the music took him over, he felt better. Today, that happened much sooner than it usually did. About five minutes after he began to play, someone dropped a five-dollar bill into his case. Isaac raised his eyes from the ground, nearly messing up his strumming to see who had been so generous. On a normal day, he considered himself lucky to get a single dollar, let alone anything bigger than that.

"Thank you!" he called after the woman.

She smiled over her shoulder as she walked away, and Isaac felt his confidence soar. He continued to play, and more people dropped their money into his case. He'd never seen so many green bills in one day. When he paused to gather it all up, he was greeted with a chorus of cheers and pleas for *Encores!*

He was taken aback.

"T-thank you, everyone!" he blubbered and fumbled awkwardly to gather his guitar back into a playing position.

He'd never had a crowd before. At most, he was used to

people going out of their way to *not* make eye contact. No one had ever stopped what they were doing to acknowledge his music. He felt good. His words weren't slurred with alcohol, and his eyes were bright with excitement. For a little while, he felt like a different person. A better person. A *happier* person.

Isaac stayed in that bliss for two hours. When the crowd finally started to disperse, and his guitar case was once again filled with bills, he decided to pack up for the night and head home, eager to count his earnings.

"The guitar is really working for you now," a voice said as Isaac snapped the case closed.

It was the man from last night, the man Isaac had tried to convince himself didn't exist. He wore the same hat and jacket, his face still shadowy despite standing in the direct line of one of the lights above.

"Yes, it has," Isaac said, forcing down the rush of apprehension that crept up his spine. "Thank you."

"I'm not here for that," the man said.

Isaac licked his teeth, slowly standing up straight so that he was eye level with the man. "What do I owe you? For your work on my guitar." He reached into his pocket to pull out a handful of bills when the man grabbed his wrist, holding him still.

"I don't want your money," he said then released him.

Isaac narrowed his eyes as he gauged the situation. If this man didn't want money, what else could there be? "What *do* you want then?" Isaac asked, shoulders slumping. Partly, he'd hoped to be able to toss some money at the man and move on with his life.

Be careful what you wish for.

MEMENTO MORI

"Come with me," he said in way of an answer and walked over to the stairs leading up and out of the subway.

Isaac hesitated. There were a lot of things that he was willing to do, but he couldn't shake the feeling in his gut that this gave him. Something wasn't right. "Uh, no offense, but if this is like a sexual thing, I don't swing that way."

"Relax," the man said, gesturing for Isaac to follow him.

Isaac wanted to do everything *but* relax. The alarm in his head told him to run, but he glanced at the case in his hand, thinking of the guitar. Not only had he fixed it, but he'd seemed to have imbibed it with some sort of power as well.

What other magic was he capable of?

Steeling his nerves, Isaac pushed away his doubts and followed. The man said nothing as he led Isaac out of the subway and into the dark neighborhood beyond. Isaac didn't recognize it and several times, he had to resist the urge to ask where they were going. He was sure the man wouldn't answer him anyway. So, Isaac followed, clutching tightly to his guitar. If the man suddenly turned on him, Isaac would be ready to swing it.

They stopped walking at the entrance of a shadowy shack.

"Do I have to go in?" Isaac asked, staying a good distance from the door in case there were others inside, waiting to ambush him.

The man patiently held the door open, a tiny smile on his face.

Licking his lips and considering his options, Isaac surrendered to his curiosity and went inside, letting the shadows engulf him. *This is stupid,* he told himself, his skin erupting in gooseflesh. The man closed the door, submerging Isaac in darkness. If he wanted to leave, it was too late now. The sounds of shuffling told him that the man was moving, and he homed in on it, keeping careful track of where he was going.

Isaac adjusted his hold on his case again and took a small step backward so that his back rested against the wall. Whatever happened here, at least it wouldn't be a sneak attack. One by one, tiny lights appeared. Candlelight. There were only a few at first, but it wasn't long before the tiny shack was filled with dozens of red candles burning, all of them different shapes and sizes.

Their combined light was enough to illuminate details about the space. Isaac's heart plummeted to his stomach when he saw what was painted on the floor in the middle of the room—a pentagram. The man was bent over it, a sharp dagger in his hand that was bigger than his palm. Beneath him was a brass collection bowl shining in the light of the fire.

"Oh," Isaac said, trying to peer through the candles to find the door. If he moved fast enough, he was sure he could push his way out and break free.

"It's okay," the man insisted, voice soothing. "Come closer, Isaac."

Isaac didn't move. "How did you know my name?"

The man grinned as if Isaac had told a great joke. "You want fame, yes? Riches?"

Isaac nodded, eyes on the knife. He'd never wanted anything more.

"I can get all that for you tonight. The success you had today is only a fraction of what I could do. Imagine a lifetime of days like today."

Isaac had never been a believer in magic before, but

maybe that had been what he was missing this entire time. Could it really be possible? He thought of his broken guitar again, how it was seamlessly fixed the next morning, and all the money inside his case now.

"It can be yours," the man said again. Isaac watched as he cut his palm, letting a thick line of crimson run into the bowl. No signs of pain showed on his face. "All I need from you is an oath."

Isaac had heard of selling his soul to get what he wanted—he'd even *joked* about it with his friends in the past—but now that the moment was before him, he froze.

"Pledge your loyalty," the man said. His voice was edgy, almost a snarl, and Isaac had a sickening premonition of what would happen if he said no.

This is everything you've ever wanted, he told himself and considered the alternative. College. A career. A family. Nothing that made life seem worthwhile.

A lifetime of fame. He closed his eyes and pictured the tiny group that had converged around him, the shouts for *encores.* That was all the motivation he needed. He dropped to his knees on the edge of the pentagram. The man urged him to hold his hand out, and Isaac obeyed. He grabbed it, his warm coppery blood sliding uncomfortably across Isaac's skin.

Isaac repressed the chill from running down his spine and tried to tell himself to not care, to let whatever happened next go down without a hitch. Taking slow breaths through his nose, the metallic tang of blood flooded his senses, reminding him that this wasn't all a terrible dream. He hoped he wouldn't pass out but had the feeling the man would take what he needed from Isaac with, or without, his consent.

KAYLA FREDERICK

The man met his eyes as he dragged the blade across Isaac's skin. Blood bubbled free, gathering in the collection bowl with the blood that was already there. As soon as the two liquids touched, the mixture began to boil. Tiny red bubbles found their way to the surface.

The man let go of Isaac and bowed his head. Subtly, Isaac backed away as the concoction frothed over the edge of the bowl and onto the floor. When the man looked up a minute later, the bleeding in his palm stopped and his eyes were black.

"It is complete."

MEMENTO MORI

3.

~1 year later~

ISAAC STARED AT his reflection in the dressing room mirror, making sure his hair was perfect. He spiked it with his fingers before pulling on his collar, tightening it. The contrast of his almost white skin to his black hair and clothes was so striking he could hardly get over his own reflection.

"You look good, sweetie," the lanky girl on the sofa beside him cooed. She tipped her head, scattering her long brown hair over the arm of the furniture as she smiled at him through exaggerated lipstick.

For the life of him, he couldn't remember her name, but it didn't matter. In a day or two, he'd be in a new town with a new girl, preparing for a new concert.

Life was good.

"Two minutes until curtain," their publicist said, peeking into the room to catch Isaac's eye.

"That's our cue," Isaac's bass guitarist, Weston, said. He was an enormous man with muscle and plenty of tattoos. His signature was his red mohawk, and the star tattooed on his cheek.

Out of all his bandmates, he was the one Isaac felt closest too. It was strange to think that a year ago, he hadn't known any of them. Now, he couldn't imagine life without them. Especially Weston. They were like his brothers, and to think of a time before they had been in his life was weird.

Isaac waved to the girl on the couch and grabbed his

guitar. He no longer used the black and gold acoustic he'd admired for such a large portion of his life. He'd swapped it in for a sleek electric model, perfect for the music his band adored. When they grouped on the stage, Isaac stood center stage, staring out across the mass of screaming fans. He adjusted his guitar, the movement scraping the scar on his palm.

His life was so different now than it had been when the scar was fresh. And so far, there'd been no negative side effects—none that he could see at least. Living without a soul seemed to treat him better than living with one ever had. He had good friends, he had adoring fans, and he had more money than he ever knew what to do with.

"Good evening, Chicago!" Isaac yelled into the microphone. His fans erupted into cheers. He grabbed it, lips brushing the surface as he added, "You ready to rock?"

More cheers.

He waited, letting the sweetness of it all wash over him. On a backward count from three, his band launched into a song, and Isaac was on cloud nine. There had been so many nights of rehearsing this song, late nights composing the rhythm, and magical moments of creating the lyrics. Isaac's heart leaked from his fingertips with every note.

He swayed to the music, and his fans sang along. Then his bandmates stopped playing. When Isaac realized it, he looked back at them then the audience. He had to squint to see past the floodlights and into the stadium. The last of the crowd was making its way through the emergency exits. Five bodies littered the ground, spread out in a way that seemed random, pointless, until Isaac's eyes moved to the center of the pit.

MEMENTO MORI

The man from the subway grinned up at Isaac.

"Dude!" Weston shrieked, dropping his guitar with a loud screech.

"What happened?" his drummer, Compton, asked, running to the edge of the stage to peer into the shadows beyond the lights.

"I-I don't know," Isaac said feeling as if he had a lump growing in his throat, making it hard to breathe.

Compton was the one to call 911 as Isaac sat on the edge of the stage, ears ringing. The strange man continued to stare at him, smiling, before vanishing in a wisp of smoke. When the police arrived, no one knew what to say. They pulled each of the members aside for questioning, but all of them had the same answer—they didn't know what had happened.

Isaac watched the bodies being loaded onto stretchers with guilt in his stomach.

4.

"WHAT DO YOU think happened?" Weston asked, plopping down on the couch in their hotel suite.

"I don't know," Isaac forced himself to say. His voice was squeaky and high, and he expected his bandmates to call him out on it.

They didn't.

"One minute, it was good, and the next? Not good," Compton said, tossing his drumsticks to the floor with a clatter.

"Do the police know how they died?" Weston asked.

"If they do, they're not saying," Compton said.

"Why focus on it? That's not gonna make us feel better," Isaac said, almost irritated that they kept the conversation going.

"Are you okay?" Weston asked.

Isaac breathed out through his nose. He didn't want to tell them the truth. If he had his way, he wouldn't. "I need to get some sleep."

"Well, I need to get *drunk*," Weston said.

Isaac didn't wait to see if they would question him further before he went into the adjoining room, enjoying the silence when the door closed behind him. His brain felt like static so he switched on the television, but there was nothing on the news. Desperate for updates, Isaac grabbed the phone off the stand, dialing the hospital.

He didn't want to believe the strange man had been there. It would be easier to accept that this was an unfortunate accident, but deep down, he knew better than that. Whatever had happened

MEMENTO MORI

to those people had somehow been Isaac's fault.

The first few times he called, there was no information. On the fourth or fifth try, Isaac learned all five people had mysteriously died of heart failure. They had been healthy upon entering the concert, but their hearts had mysteriously failed within a short span of one another.

You killed them, a voice whispered in the back of his head. *They would be alive if it wasn't for you.*

People die, he argued back and laid down on the bed, holding a pillow over his face in an attempt to block everything out. In the darkness, there were flashes of the bodies, the concert, the *man*. Isaac jumped up, searching his luggage for a tiny bottle of vodka. Maybe Weston was right about getting drunk. He finished it in two big sips and lay back down, staring at the ceiling with the tingly feeling of movement throughout his body.

In the realm of dreams, the man's face was the first thing Isaac saw. Closing his eyes, he tried to drown it all out, but the man was still there. He detached himself from the shadows, stalking closer.

"Was it you?" Isaac asked, holding his head high.

The man's smile widened as if he fed off Isaac's pain, anger, and fear. "No, my dear boy. It was all *you*."

Isaac woke in a cold sweat, panting. It felt as if there were invisible hands wrapped around his throat, squeezing the life out of him. Isaac scratched his skin, finally able to draw in a deep breath. Weston, who was sitting at the table on the other side of their shared room, glanced over to him. "Everything alright, mate?"

"Yeah, fine," Isaac said and ruffled his hair. "I'm ready to get out of this Godforsaken city."

"You're not the only one," Weston said, snapping the clasps on his suitcase closed. "You packed?"

Isaac climbed out of bed, throwing on the nearest outfit and shoving the rest into his suitcase. "Ready."

He said nothing of the nightmare as he and his bandmates boarded the tour bus. Isaac was glad that it was still dark. It was easy to drown himself in alcohol and pass out again. If any of his bandmates sensed anything was off about him, they said nothing.

IN THE NEXT city, Isaac wasn't woken by his publicist or any of his bandmates. There were groupies on the bus. A blonde girl who appeared to be about five years younger than him made eye contact with him. Despite the dark feelings in his heart, he kissed her, losing himself in her warmth and the heavy scent of her perfume. After they had sex, he felt a bit better. Enough that Weston was able to get him into the concert hall. Subtly, he pulled Isaac aside by the elbow.

"Are you sure you're alright?" he asked.

"Yeah, I'm good."

"I know last night was rough. It's gonna take us all some time to get over, but it's going to be okay," Weston said.

"Yeah, yeah," Isaac said, shouldering past him to follow the rest of the band inside. He didn't have the heart to point out that Weston was playing with forces outside of his control, that he had no way of *knowing* that things would be okay

Isaac appreciated the sentiment.

In the dressing room, Isaac kept away the new wave of

MEMENTO MORI

groupies by pretending to rehearse. He was sure Weston would be able to see through his act, but he didn't ask him anymore questions.

"Five minutes," their publicist called.

Weston patted Isaac on the shoulder as they made their way out to the stage. As they took their places, Isaac told himself to breathe, that everything was going to be alright, but his anxiety began to climb once again. The people amassed in the auditorium called for him, shouting their love and support. Isaac scanned the unfamiliar faces, pausing when he saw the man in the front row, grinning up at him.

The greeting he was supposed to deliver lodged in his throat, and Weston covered for him. The crowd cheered, not noticing the slip up as they began to play. All of them except for Isaac. He was frozen, staring into the man's eyes. His heart pounded harder and harder, feeling as if it was swelling inside of his chest, ready to give out like the five victims in their last concert.

He screamed, "No! Stop!"

It was too late.

Excitement changed to horror. The first body fell and as Isaac's eyes moved around the crowd, he saw the other four join in. Terrified wails erupted, and the audience spread out, dispersing until only five bodies remained. Isaac was comatose as his eyes moved from one to the other. It was worse this time, worse because he had made sure to glimpse the life in their eyes before it was snuffed out for good.

Weston called the police, and when they arrived, there was less bafflement and more suspicion. To have this happen once was a sad and tragic event but twice was not something the police would accept. The manager of the auditorium and Isaac's publicist were pulled aside first as the band was separated and questioned.

Again, they all had the same lack of knowledge. Cameras cleared them of suspicion by showing that they hadn't left the stage the entire time. By the end of the night, the police had nothing they could do except escort the band back to their hotel rooms.

The press ate it up.

The news that night informed Isaac he'd been branded the Killer Singer. His concerts were *to die for*. Isaac squeezed his eyes closed as he watched the headlines, wishing it all away. He now knew the horrible price his life cost—it wasn't just *his* soul that he had bargained. He had offered up innocent souls as well.

Isaac forced himself to go to sleep with the aid of a heavy tonic of alcohol, ready for what the void on the other side would bring.

"How do I end this?" Isaac yelled into the black void of his nightmares.

No response.

Angry, Isaac balled his hands into fists and marched through the darkness, not caring that every step he took got him nowhere. He shouted and cursed until the shadows shifted, gathering into the man who leered at him. Every time he appeared, his features seemed tighter, less friendly, and Isaac wondered if the human façade would fade completely. "Isaac, whatever seems to be the problem?"

"You know exactly what my problem is," Isaac fumed, jabbing his finger into the man's ugly coat. "You already knew what would happen if I agreed to your deal, and you never told

MEMENTO MORI

me."

The man lifted his chin, waiting for Isaac to continue.

"I...I want it to stop," Isaac said. "You've taken enough."

"But you have everything you've ever dreamed of."

"You never said innocent people would be killed," Isaac said, voice dropping to a whisper as his mind replayed the image of the bodies falling to the floor.

"I never said they *wouldn't* be either. You assumed. Just as you assumed you would be able to pay the cost of your dreams."

"It doesn't matter what happened then. I know the truth now so tell me...how do I make it stop?" Isaac demanded, breathless.

"I think you know," the man said. "You either live with your dream or die without it."

KAYLA FREDERICK

5.

ISAAC ONCE AGAIN woke in a clammy sweat. He didn't move, lying still in bed with details of his dream at the front of his brain. This wouldn't stop—it would never stop. For him to be successful, to have the life he always dreamed of, other people had to die.

Isaac bit his lip, trying to calm himself. *I can deal with this.* When he'd made the deal, Isaac had considered the possibility that *someone* would die, and he'd made his peace with it. Back then, he had been willing to *kill* someone to see his dreams come true.

After a year of living it up, it was easy to forget the raw determination that had led him here, the desperation. The *heartbreak*. If he had been that willing at one point then the desire was still in him somewhere. And it wasn't as if he had to kill anyone himself. People would never know. Not to mention the fact that they were *strangers*. If he didn't think about it too hard, then it hardly mattered.

That morning, his bandmates said very little about what had happened. All he had to do was stay quiet. Pretend to be like them. Partially, Isaac wondered if there was a reason why *these* people had flocked to be his bandmates. He knew them, but suddenly, he realized he didn't know them *well*. Part of him started to suspect that maybe they had made deals too.

What if they had *all* sold their souls?

Whatever they case, if they weren't disturbed by what happened, Isaac wouldn't let himself be either.

He got himself ready for another concert. He sorted

through all his black leather outfits, picking the one that would stand out the least. No doubt he'd have enough attention falling on himself without calling for it.

"I can't believe this," Weston said from the tiny common area of the bus. The television was on, the news playing.

Isaac barely wanted to know what he was talking about. Against his better judgment, he trudged over to sit beside his friend. The news was talking about his band, the last two concerts they had attended, and the ten people Isaac was sure he had killed. He expected the report to be full of negativity and hate, but it was the opposite. People were raving on the internet for tickets, some of them going so far as to hunt down people who *did* have tickets. It seemed the deaths had given his band *more* attention which meant *more* fans. A sick sort of marketing gig.

Isaac swallowed roughly, thinking of the smiling man in the middle of the bodies. This was the payoff. Isaac had held up his end of the bargain by providing victims, and the man would hold up his end by continuing to make Isaac's dream a reality. Isaac, as well as his bandmates, were rising in fame. At the rate Isaac was going, he would be in the Hall of Fame before he was thirty.

Despite his earlier promise that he would come to terms with his life, he couldn't do it. He sought out the cabinet, pulling out another tiny bottle of vodka. He downed it in one gulp, letting the warmth wash over him. The warm buzz of alcohol didn't assuage the guilt, so he chased it with another one. His head filled with the sensation of rushing water, his legs swaying beneath him. The second bottle made it easier to deal with things, and to make sure, he grabbed a third and tucked it away into his pocket before he turned to go back to his room.

"Dude, are you drunk? It's not even noon," Weston chastised.

"Drop it," Isaac slurred, too busy focusing on walking to engage in the argument.

"You gotta relax," Weston said. "What happened sucks but drinking yourself away isn't going to make anything better."

"More people want to come to our concerts," Isaac managed to say and pointed at the television. The news had switched to reporting on something else, but Weston grunted in understanding anyway.

"It's crazy, *people* are crazy, but what happened…it isn't our fault," Weston shrugged. "You know how people are. They probably OD'd on something."

"The autopsy reports would've picked up on that in at least *one* of them. Two concerts? Five people at each, and no answers?" If Isaac had been sober, he would've kept all of that to himself, but in his inebriated state, it felt important to lay it all out, to see if anyone else would come to the conclusion that he was a monster.

Weston lit a cigarette, taking a deep puff before he blew it out. "Yeah, it's all weird, but what's done is done. Maybe our next concert will be better."

MEMENTO MORI

6.

ISAAC REALLY WANTED Weston's words to be true, wanted the incidents to be nothing more than an ugly coincidence, but he knew better. That familiar feeling of anxiety wiggled into his brain as he took his place on stage. Gripping tightly to his guitar, Isaac stared down into the faces of his fans with tears in his eyes. He wasn't drunk anymore, but the lingering effects of alcohol were still there, unlocking parts of him that he wished were still hidden.

Who am I going to kill today? he asked himself as he scanned their faces.

Isaac had told Weston in advance that he didn't want to do the intro this time. Maybe if he backed off, if someone *else* took the spotlight, then maybe someone wouldn't have to die. Isaac let himself fall into the background, taking a few steps backward so that Weston was the most prominent figure on stage. When they made it through the first half of the set, Isaac started to let himself believe that everything was going to be okay.

The love for music he used to have, before he became a different person, was restored. Like a caterpillar emerging from a cocoon, he came out of his paranoia and started to dance around like he usually did. His fans clapped and cheered, so loudly that he hardly noticed the new sound—the thump of a guitar smacking against the ground.

He turned in the same second Weston faceplanted on the stage.

Isaac forgot how to breathe. If he'd been any closer to the edge, he might've fallen right off. Blackness took over his peripheral as his vision went narrow. He fell to his knees beside his fallen friend, watching as the tunnel of his vision closed to pinholes then was consumed by blackness.

WHEN ISAAC OPENED his eyes again, he wasn't sure if he'd blacked out or if he'd died beside his friend. Isaac was nowhere near the concert. He was in the old shack, the one where he had given his oath. He couldn't see the man in the shadows but felt him nearby.

"I didn't think it would be someone I know," Isaac said, somehow keeping the tremor out of his voice.

"I made no such promises," the voice snarled from the darkness.

"I want it to stop."

The man's sharp features appeared carved into something wicked as he stared into Isaac's eyes. "Then you know what you must do."

MEMENTO MORI

7.

"SUCH A SHAME," Officer Garrison said to the Detective beside him. "He was young, had everything going for him."

Detective Wellson stared at the body hanging from the rope. The head was down, face angled to the floor. By the purple marks on his neck and stiffness of his hands into claws—as well as the bluish tips of his fingers—it was clear he'd suffocated. And it had taken him a long time to die.

"Why do these types do anything that they do?" Officer Garrison continued.

"I don't know, but this was no ordinary rockstar. This was the Killer Singer," Detective Wellson said.

"Heh. Ironic choice of a name."

"I don't think it was *his* choice."

"Whatever. Let's just get him cut down."

Carefully, they worked to free the body from the rope, laying it onto the stretcher that had been brought in a few minutes prior. One mangled hand slipped off the edge, knuckles thumping onto the floor. Detective Wellson put it back in place, staring at the contrast of the blue fingers to the white scar across his palm.

KAYLA FREDERICK

MEMENTO MORI

A kind soul is gradually destroyed by a world of cruelty.

KAYLA FREDERICK

MEMENTO MORI

When it Comes

CORA MOVED AROUND the dark interior of her kitchen with practiced steps. Candlelight flickered from a rapidly diminishing candle on the middle of the table, but the light it threw was small and weak. The sun had made its final descent beneath the horizon sometime during Cora's meager meal, and with it, her better candle had gone out as well.

This tiny thing was all she had left, the only light until she could figure out a way to afford to get a new one. Lips pressed together, she gathered her bowl and spoon, sticky with remaining traces of soup. Seemed it had been ages since she'd had any leftovers.

Have I ever?

She dropped the utensils into the wooden bucket that sat beside the front door intending to wash them in the morning then make her rounds.

Hopefully I'll be able to get food and *a new candle,* she thought, unsure which one she'd choose if it came down to it. She could live in the dark for a few days, but hunger?

That was harder.

Cora picked up a rag and started to clean the table, trying to distract herself. There used to be a time, when she was a young girl, that she would've been ashamed of this life where she depended so heavily on others' generosity to survive. Cora observed the fine wrinkles beginning to show on the back of her hands. Once, she'd been a prominent maiden with dozens of suitors and the world had been her oyster. Now all she had was regret. Not a day went by without her cursing her younger self. The girl who had turned down a real future over something as petty as a man's hairline.

Cora adjusted the waistband of her dark yellow kirtle dress, feeling how sunken and tiny her abdomen had become. It wasn't a healthy kind of skinny. If she didn't put some weight on soon, there was a good chance she wouldn't make it through winter.

Cora grabbed the chamberstick, and the candlelight flickered, threatening to go out. She paused, giving it a second to correct itself before she made a move to leave the room. A pronounced knock on the door gave her pause. It came as three loud taps. The kind she would expect from someone of importance.

When she glanced toward the window, she was once again reminded of the late hour, and the fact that important men didn't travel after dark. They stayed holed up in their homes, safe and sound, until the sun would rise again in the morning and chase away the monsters of the night.

Cora steeled her shoulders but didn't make a move to open it. A few other homes in the village had been robbed recently, and she wondered if the culprits had finally made their way to her doorstep.

Joke's on them. If they came inside, they'd leave disappointed.

Just as she did every day.

MEMENTO MORI

Pounding came from the door again, and Cora twitched her nose, waiting for it to stop.

Bang.

Bang.

Bang.

The last one was by far the longest and most drawn out as if whoever was on the other side knew she had no plans to open it and considered busting it down to get in.

Cora took one step backward, and an odd moaning seeped into the still night air. Deep and throaty, it made her think of a beast rather than a man.

Against her better judgement, Cora called, "Who's there?"

"Let…me…in," the thing said in a series of croaks and grunts so animalistic she barely understood it.

Heart pounding, she pressed her slight frame against the door, knowing that if this thing wanted to break in, her weight wouldn't be enough to stop it.

"Don't you think it's rude to intrude on a lady's place of rest once the sun is down?" she called, hoping this was all a prank that would end soon if she seemed like too much of a challenge.

"So…*hungry*," the thing rasped and banged on the door.

Something wiggled up her belly, an emotion she'd long since stopped feeling. Cold, tactical *anger*. She had next to nothing, but the few possessions she *did* own, food included, she'd *earned*. Who was this person to take it from her?

"I don't have anything for you!" she hollered loud enough that her throat felt raspy.

Silence.

That scared her more than its noises. Had it left? She couldn't tell and feared getting too close to the window. Cora's mouth filled with saliva in a way that could've been preparing her to fight or flee.

A shriek blasted the night, so forceful and violent it rattled the entire door.

"Food! I need food!" the thing screamed over and over. The more it repeated the phrase, the more human it began to sound.

It didn't take long for Cora to forget the gravelly screeches she'd first heard. For her to forget the primal fear this creature's appearance had stirred in her and reignite her anger. Switching the candle to her non-dominant hand, she pulled the door open.

The thing on her stoop was humanoid in shape, but that was where the similarities between it and a person ended. The body was a dark mess of shadows, the arms ending in a spray of twisting black tentacles. More of them sprouted from his shoulders. The head was tipped to the side, the mouth open to reveal a neon green tongue so vibrant, it shone in the low light of dusk. Another blast of the same color radiated in the middle of its chest. Two red diamonds stared from the top of the black mass.

As soon as their eyes met, Cora couldn't move. She wanted to scream, to run for the moors, *anything*, but she'd lost control of her body. Black haze encroached the edges of her vision, and the world tilted before fading away.

**

WHEN CORA OPENED her eyes, she gasped so loud, she was sure everyone in her village overheard. Shaking, she looked around until she realized she was in her room. Struggling to get her breathing under control, she pressed a hand to her forehead, wiping away the sweat.

She didn't remember going to bed. She'd been cleaning the kitchen and plotting her plans for the morning when...Cora couldn't remember *what* had happened.

Thrusting the blanket aside, she realized she still wore the dress she'd had on the night before. It wasn't uncommon for the other beggars in the village to wear the same outfit for days at a time, but she'd always vowed not be like them. She only possessed a few sparse outfits, but she washed and changed as much as possible. it was the only part of her vanity left from her maidenhood.

Skin still crawling with the aftereffects of a nightmare she couldn't remember, she made her way across the room and plucked a clean dress from the closet. Once dressed, she tossed her soiled outfit into the bucket with her dirty dishes.

Cora knelt down to scoop it up when a great cramp seized her stomach. Her entire abdomen rattled with the kind of hunger that usually came from missing a few meals.

That soup was little more than water, she reasoned. It made sense she'd be hungry again already.

Tucking the bucket against her hip, Cora stepped

outside to find the sun high in the sky. *How long did I sleep?*

Squinting, she made her way down the dirt path and into the heart of the village, passing a few homes, the front yards littered with makeshift shops. The owners watched her from the shadows created by the blankets they'd hung up to keep the sunlight off them. Cora did her best to pretend she didn't notice.

On an ordinary day, she woke and began her day when the sun barely peeked above the horizon. As a result, she didn't get as many sour looks passing through town and stood a better chance of securing offerings later on in the evening. Other townsfolk, the ones milling from shop to shop, avoided eye contact with her as if she were one of the stray dogs who occasionally wandered in from the moors.

The simple gesture used to be enough to hurt Cora's feelings, to make her feel less than everyone else. They stirred nothing in her now. It was part of being a beggar. She'd long ago become a pest, an inconvenience.

Cora kept her gaze on the path ahead. Several more houses sat between her and the woods that led to the creek, then she'd be out of sight. On instinct, she glanced at the door of one of the homes as she walked by, but the door didn't open, and Cora continued on her way.

The woman who lived there was perhaps the closest thing to family that Cora had left. Or at the very least, she was a sympathetic ear she could depend on in times of hardship. Agnes had once been a friend of her mother's. When things had taken a turn for the worse, Agnes had been there. After Cora's mother passed, she'd offered what support she could despite the fact she was a mere spinster herself.

Spinster.

The ugly word bounced around the inside of Cora's head. She hated that term. Hated the ugly implications that came with it as if being on her own somehow made her less than other women her age who were married and had a family.

Cora peeked back to see if Agnes had noticed her, but she hadn't. She continued down the slope and into the woods, the smooth dirt path underfoot changing to rough stones as it dumped her at the edge of a brook.

The village maidens had already made their rounds to bathe, leaving only a few tired women cleaning the last bit of their clothing. Cora sank into her favorite spot in the shadow of a towering oak. A soft breeze ruffled her dark locks as she took her soiled dress from the bucket. In the direct sunlight, it was dirty with several tears as if she'd spent the night aimlessly wandering through the woods and forgotten the journey upon returning home.

How odd.

She sank it beneath the surface of the burbling stream. Pinning it in place with one hand, she used her other to pry one of the stones from the creek bed and pounded it against the dress over and over again, cautious of the places where it had begun to tear. Satisfied with her work, she pulled the dress out, squeezing out the excess water.

Most of the stains had come out except for one particularly prominent black smudge right beneath the neckline. Cora ran her finger over the splotch. *What is that?* She didn't remember where it had come from. She dunked the dress again, finding a different stone to take over the job of cleaning, but the stubborn stain remained.

Cora was ready to throw it in for a third wash when a painful cramp seized her stomach, making her drop it. She pitched forward, wrapping her arms around her abdomen. Her body rioted with pain as if a large creature had burrowed down into the depths of her organs and now wanted out. She thought wistfully of the food she'd eaten the night before and wondered if there had been something wrong with it. When she'd been given the stew from the owner of the inn, she'd been grateful, but now, she wondered if there had been a reason behind his generosity.

Pain rippled through her, changing to a more familiar sensation—hunger. Cora's hands shook with it. She scanned the nearby bushes for berries, and when she saw none, the grass beneath her became a feasible option.

What is wrong with you? she chastised.

Trying to compose herself, she picked up her dress and brushed away the clinging traces of leaves and debris. She couldn't be certain, but for a second, she would've sworn the black smudge glowed green.

***

CORA FINISHED HER wash and dropped her bucket back at home before going into town carrying one small clay cup with her. It was the last of her mother's belongings she owned.

Besides her house of course.

Walking in zombie-like steps through the same path

MEMENTO MORI

she'd taken earlier in the day, Cora held the cup up. The sun had already begun its descent, pink-red light bathing familiar surroundings in its eerie tint. Shop owners ignored her, pretending they were busy closing for the day rather than make some excuse directly to her face about why they couldn't spare any coins.

Worming pains crawled through her stomach, and she feared the onset of another spasm of the same caliber as the one that had crippled her at the creek. A red apple at the nearest booth caught her eye, and she shook her cup, rattling the few coins inside. It wasn't enough. Cora knew that, but desperation had her run up to the stall anyway.

The girl behind it appeared to be barely eighteen. With wide eyes, she stared at Cora. Cora had met her in church before, but she couldn't remember her name and didn't care enough about niceties to pretend she did.

"Can I-I have this?" she asked, pointing to the apple that had beckoned her from across the plaza.

"No, you—" the girl tried to say.

Cora lost focus, gaze dropping to the spread of fruit that separated them. There were apples, potatoes, and far more other vegetables than one person needed. *They won't miss one apple*, she reasoned and dove for it.

The second her teeth pierced the flesh, the girl took her escape. Cora could hear her calling for help, but it seemed like a distant problem as she devoured the soft pulp. The flavor sang on her tongue, and she ate down to the core. On second thought, she ate that too.

The rumbling in her stomach eased slightly, and she

began to lick the sticky juices off her fingers, desperate to clean them, when angry voices made her turn. The girl was coming back with an older man in tow. Her father, Alban. The one who had grown the stolen product.

"That's her!" the woman shouted.

Cora took a step backward, knowing she had no way to defend herself.

"Aye, lass! What's the matter with ye?" Alban yelled as he approached. "Scaring my girl all ova' an apple? You oughta be ashamed!"

And she was.

So very, very ashamed, but she couldn't explain what had driven her to do it. The hunger that had made her lose control.

"Ye' Campbells are all insane," he continued dismissively. "Your mother was a peach. But ye? They shoulda run ye out of town a long time ago!"

Cora didn't realize she was on the verge of crying until cool water streaked her cheek. Sniffling, she took a step backward, but she couldn't bring herself to run. "I-I—" she floundered.

"Aye, what's going on ova' here?" a new voice, a *familiar* voice called from the shadows between the nearby houses.

Cora's heart skipped a beat, and she couldn't decide if it came from relief or the crushing disappointment that out of all people to see her at this lowest possible moment of her life, it would be Agnes.

Cold, thin fingers wrapped around her upper arm,

pulling her back from the angry farmer as Agnes interjected herself between them. She was in her years and walked with a totter, but she had a surprising amount of strength left in her.

"What's it to ya?" Alban quibbled. "This be between me a' the thief!"

"Thief?" she asked, turning a questioning eye to Cora.

Cora bowed her head, somehow more ashamed than she'd been earlier.

"Woman stole me produce. Poor Anabella was terrified!"

"Where's your humanity?" Agnes chastised. "Clearly, she's starvin'! You'll do fine without one tiny piece of fruit."

Alban sneered. "Thieves *deserve* to go hungry, if ye as' me."

Agnes cut her eyes at him before she pulled a coin purse from the folds of her dark dress. "'ere. Take a few coins and be on ye way."

Alban watched mistrustfully. When Agnes summoned actual money, his hand shot out, palm up. Agnes dropped the coins, and he sorted them with his thumb, carefully counting before he squeezed his hand shut. With narrowed eyes, he peered up at Agnes then Cora.

"Next time, I won' leave so easy," he said and wrapped his arm over his daughter's shoulders.

Agnes and Cora stayed silent as the two farmers stood in front of their booth, eyeing the women. Agnes guided her down the path and out of the plaza, away from the scene of the crime. Cora's skin crawled with all the possibilities of what Agnes might say.

"Now tha' we're alone, tell me wha' tha' was about," Agnes said, tucking her coin purse away. Her voice wasn't angry or concerned. It was curious, *cautious*.

"I was...*hungry*," Cora said. It was the honest truth, and yet, it still felt as if she were lying. She wouldn't put into words exactly what had clawed at her brain and compelled her to act so hastily.

Agnes' deep blue eyes stared at her, red-rimmed and sad. She had a gleam about her that Cora had never noticed before, almost a haze that reminded her of the stress she'd seen in her mother's eyes before the sickness had taken over.

"Let's get ye home."

***

BACK IN THE safety of her own kitchen, Cora wasn't sure what to do. Agnes brought her comfort, but Cora wasn't used to having other people in her home. She pulled out a rickety wooden chair, and Agnes sat on it, looking around, taking in things Cora couldn't see, memories that had passed long ago.

Cora sat down across her from, still shaking from the incident with Alban.

"Ye've gotte' thinner," Agnes said when Cora drew a blank for conversation starters.

"Life hasn't...gotten easier," she admitted and stared at the oncoming night outside. In the distance, an eerie howl broke the quiet, and she imagined wolves picking their way through the fields, hunting sheep in their own cycles of desperate hunger.

"Ye can't live this way forever, child," Agnes said.

Cora dug her fingers into the table, finding it harder and harder to focus on the conversation as her vision swirled. She propped her head up, using her dwindling energy to try and keep eye contact.

"It's not forever, it's—"

"Ye don't look good," Agnes interjected.

Cora's stomach rumbled, and unlike before, this didn't feel like hunger, but *vomit*. Her hand went to her mouth, and understanding dawned on Agnes' face. She grabbed the bucket of clean dishes Cora had dropped by the door and tipped it upside down, emptying the contents onto the table.

"Here."

Queasy, Cora took it, but nothing came up. Her stomach felt hollow, empty in a way she'd never felt before. She willed the sensation to pass. Agnes simpered and sat back down, attention going to the dress rumpled on the table. The wettest parts of the fabric drooped when she held it up, better observing it in the candlelight.

"Wha's this?" Agnes asked, touching the stain Cora had been unable to remove.

Cora stared at it, unwilling to say. After today, the last thing she wanted was to tell Agnes that she didn't *know* what it was or what had happened to her the night before.

Agnes set the dress down, and Cora peeked up at her. A fresh look of horror washed over the woman, an expression Cora had never seen her wear.

"Wha' is it?"

"Wha's happened to ye?" Agnes asked in a soft

whisper. She looked down at the stain again then back at Cora. "Please tell me you weren't visited by the Hungry One."

"The...Hungry One?"

"Our ancesto's called it the *Fear Gorta*," Agnes clarified. "A creature capable of blessin' a peasant with riches an' tearing down the wealthiest te beggars."

"It's not real. Tha's a legend," Cora stated. "Mom used to say the creature would ta'e me away if I didn't finish dinner."

Agnes pressed her lips into a straight line, grim in a way that assured Cora this wasn't some joke. This woman, who she cherished, wasn't playing a joke on her.

Agnes poked the stain again. "This says otherwise."

"If it... came 'ere, I don't rememba'. All I can say about last night is that I was eatin' dinner then I wo'e up in bed. The entire nigh' is a blank space in me memory."

"Did you deny it food?"

Cora narrowed her eyes to slits, wondering how well Agnes was actually listening. "I told ye, I don't *remember*."

The grim expression grew bleaker. "Well, let's hope you didn't. When it comes, ye should neve' deny its request. Treat it with kindness or be cursed to a life of regret."

Cora didn't have the heart to tell her that was already how she lived. "Wha' happens if...if this thing *did* come 'ere last night? And hypothetically, I *did* turn it down?"

"Ye'll be cursed with a hunger so severe it'll ruin ye," she said.

As if to prove her right, Cora's stomach grumbled, a sharp stab of hunger coming with it. Agnes' words faded away to a haze of sounds as Cora lifted her hand. She waved it back and forth, watching her fingers part and come together as if it was disconnected from her body. She shoved the side of her fist into her mouth and bit down. Hard. Her brittle teeth cracked from the pressure, and her knuckles smashed together. Over the taste of the blood, she felt no pain. Cora loosened her grip and went for another bite, this time from the meaty part of her forearm.

Agnes lunged so fast she nearly knocked the entire table over. They wrestled, Agnes trying to hold her head in place while Cora gnashed and snapped her teeth. The second she knocked Agnes off, she went for the bite. Her flesh was salty, coppery where the blood touched it, but it was softer than her hand had been. Cora turned her head to the side, nearly freeing the chunk when something pulled her hair, wrenching her head backward.

Cora bit the air, like a wild animal, her teeth making an awful clacking sound. Agnes shoved something into Cora's flailing jaws, ceasing her attacks. Sweet juices ran into her mouth. She hesitated then took one bite and another, slumping in Agnes' grip as she finished the fruit in rapid bites. When it was gone, she nipped her fingertips and cold consciousness returned.

She blinked, groggy as if she'd woken from a deep sleep. Agnes held a white cloth over Cora's forearm. Patches of red leaked through it. A matching stream ran from the side of her hand.

Wide-eyed, she looked up at Agnes. "Wh-what happened?"

Agnes' lips pushed into that grim line again, and Cora wondered if she was stuck with that expression. "I'm afraid ye've got the Hunger."

Cora wanted to be mad at her, to feel something other than the terrified hopelessness the situation had left her with, but she couldn't.

"It's no' real," she said pathetically. She didn't know what she thought could happen by denying it, but accepting it was downright insane.

Maybe I am too.

Agnes lifted her rag, revealing the clotted blood that had gathered underneath. With the water diluting it, it ran in thin streams, exaggerating the seriousness. "Looks pretty real ta me."

Cora forced herself to stare at the laceration ringed with teeth marks. Those were *her* teeth marks.

"Wha' do I do?"

Agnes sighed, loud and long, staring out into the shadows as if they could help her handle the situation. "There is a way te break the curse," she began slowly, as if she were testing the words in her mouth before giving them legs. "But it's a long shot."

"Wha' is it?" Cora asked, sniffling. "I'll do anything." And it was true. If there was a way to never feel that dreadful hunger again, she would cut off her own leg.

"The *Fear Gorta* is a being closely entwined with nature. If ye salt and burn its sacred ground, it will perish, and ye'll be free."

"B-but how do I know where tha' is?" Cora asked. She

felt like a little kid again, clueless and dependent on someone older and wiser to keep her safe.

"Ye don't. That's why it's a long shot."

***

LYING IN BED that night, Cora dissolved into tears. Agnes had carefully dressed her wounds the best she could with her meager supplies. She'd also taken it upon herself to wrap Cora's arms in soft towels in case she lost control again.

Not a matter of if but when, she reminded herself when she remembered all Agnes had said.

The *Hunger*.

She closed her eyes, trying to recall anything from her missing night but was unsuccessful.

Maybe it's for the best I can't remember. She stared at the dressing over her wounded arm. Something that could drive her to this wouldn't be pretty if it got worse.

A deep piercing howl drifted through her window from the moors, and Cora shivered. The beasts around the village were always hungry. They roamed all hours of the day, searching for any unfortunate animals they could pick off. Many nights she'd heard the death wails of their victims.

Cora bolted up in bed, staring out into the starless night with a renewed sense of clarity.

The *moors*.

Like the other stray animals that found the village, the creature had most likely come from there. If that was the case, its sacred land was out there *somewhere*.

KAYLA FREDERICK

Cora threw herself out of bed so fast she nearly caught her foot in the blanket and fell. Breathing heavily, she caught her balance and scooped up her chamberstick. The candle had gone out, but she relit it and made her way to the dining room. On the way, she grabbed a clean linen towel. She set down the chamberstick and knocked everything off the table with a massive *crash* before she laid out her towel. She scooped up a pouch with a few clinging traces of salt in it along with her flint and steel and set them in a pile.

Cora studied the items with wariness. *If anyone sees me traveling with this, they're going to think I'm a witch.* Her stomach rumbled, and she groaned. *I'm dead either way.*

She grabbed the edges of the towel, trapping everything inside as she hauled the bundle over her shoulder. She made a move to grab her chamberstick but stopped. The winds on the moors would do away with the tiny flame quickly.

Bracing herself, she slipped outside, listening to her door rattle behind her. The night air was still and soft, a bit of moonlight falling to the ground from the claw scratch of the moon, and it was hard to imagine that the end of her mission involved a monster she'd have to slay.

Cora stood on her stoop, contemplating her next move. She was scared, *terrified*, of being in the wilderness alone. Her mission aside, the moors weren't a tranquil place. The heather was filled with wolves and wild hounds, real animals who would gladly harm her given the opportunity.

I shouldn't go alone, she thought and stared down the dark path that led to Agnes' house. Perhaps her only ally in this life was far more fragile than she was.

If I lose control again, Agnes will only be in danger.

Cora decided she would go alone. Ultimately, that was how she'd gotten herself into this mess, right? She must have denied the creature food. The smudge on her dress, in the place above her chest, was a reminder of her own black heart.

For all the times the villagers have fed me, I had no kindness, no urge, to do the same for someone else in need.

The thought weighed her down as she plodded along the road toward the open expanse of moors. At what point had she lost her humanity? Cora couldn't define the exact moment. Once upon a time, she'd been soft, and kind, and believed in the goodness of others. Then, she'd let the darkness of her mother's passing corrupt her, used it as an excuse to isolate herself, to take the easy way out when things had gotten too hard.

Imagine that. Between me and the Hungry One, I'm the true monster.

The wind ruffled her hair, chilling her. She hugged herself tight, trying not to let the stillness of the open wild scare her. Cora's entire body buzzed with terrified anxiety when she remembered all the horror stories of field hands being eaten by wolves. If they came upon her, she wouldn't stand a chance. She looked back over her shoulder at the village she was leaving behind. It was dark too, as unwelcoming as the path ahead.

That's a bad omen, she told herself but continued on. She'd come too far to go back.

Pain as sharp as talons cut into her stomach, and she

heaved forward, nearly dropping her bag. Somehow, she kept her stuff from spilling out, but a new problem came.

She was hungry again.

The smartest move she could've made would've been to ask Agnes for some food for the trip. She wanted to bring some while packing, except she didn't have anything left.

The primal urge to bite her own flesh returned, but the bandages were too thick for Cora's teeth to pierce through. She went for her hand again, the only part of her arms that hadn't been protected. *Crunch.* The chunk of flesh went down easily. The copper scent of blood brought with it a loud piercing howl from the boughs of heather.

Two yellow eyes shone in the moonlight. Normally, Cora would be afraid of such a threat, but in her trance, she stood her ground, grinding her teeth into her own flesh defiantly. With a snarl, the creature broke from its hiding place, charging toward her in a flurry of teeth and mottled fur.

Cora swung her makeshift bag, smacking it in the side of the head. Stunned, the wolf went off course before lunging again, sinking its teeth into the fleshy underpart of her upper arm.

She kicked the creature, trying to throw it off, but she was so weak, her attack did little more than stir a fresh growl from the beast. It clamped harder, and she had the horrific image of it ripping the entire chunk of meat free.

Echoing the growl, she dropped her supplies and went for its throat. Its fur tickled her nose and filled her mouth, fuzzy against her tongue. The second her teeth pierced its flesh, it howled and let go of her arm.

MEMENTO MORI

Cora had no intention of doing the same.

Using all her force, she bit until she tasted blood. The wolf tried to bite her back, but she grabbed its snout, pushing its head to the side until its neck made a horrific *crack,* and the beast went still. Cora locked her jaws, at first drinking the blood that seeped out. When that wasn't enough to satisfy her, she pulled free a chunk of meat. It was squishy and hot, the sinews hard to chew, but she gulped it down and went for more.

She sank to her knees in the mud, adjusting her grip on the beast to rip away the meat from the shoulder. White bone gleamed in the moonlight. She kept eating until she made it to the wolf's stomach. It had been a while since the wolf's last meal, she could tell by how sunken in the creature was. She dug her fingernails into the flesh, listening to it pop and squelch as torrents of blood found their way free.

Cora pulled out a handful of wet and slimy entrails. They were chewier than the muscles had been. She swallowed them down, pulling out the liver and kidneys. By the time she was reasonably full, she'd cleaned out the wolf's entire abdominal cavity.

Warm and sticky with blood coating her chin, throat, and hands, she stared at the dead creature. She lifted her left hand then the right. Horrified, she held a hand over her mouth and stared at what she'd done.

With her bare hands, she'd taken this creature's life.

Cora had never killed anything before. When she'd been a little girl, and her mother still had her chickens, her and her siblings rotated slaughter duties. When her turn came, she'd refused. Back then, she'd rather go hungry than take the life of *anything*. She held a hand over her full belly, thinking how much the world had changed since then. How much *she* had changed.

"I'm sorry," she said to the wolf before she went to work gathering her scattered supplies.

Briefly, she considered burying the beast, but it would take too much time. Time she didn't have. Bloody and exhausted, Cora scooped the creature's hollow carcass into her arms. Sticks stuck to the muck on her legs, threatening to slow her down, but she pushed through the heather.

The wolf had heft to it; something Cora realized the longer she carried it. Her energy seemed to diminish twice as fast, and she wondered if bringing it along had been her best decision.

You're going to need it, she reminded herself.

With the smell of so much blood in the air, she worried about the possibility of attracting other predators, predators who may be bigger and harder to take down than the wolf. Her skin crawled at the idea of taking another life.

Ahead, the ground sloped toward a bare patch of dirt, leading her to the side of a tributary. This part of the river ran into the woods, trickling away to the creek she was so familiar with. Out here, the water was deeper, more dangerous.

Cora decided to follow it farther into the heather and away from civilization. A breeze stirred the foliage, masking all sounds. Shivering, she squinted, struggling to get a glimpse of what lie ahead.

A horse stable.

MEMENTO MORI

  Cora stopped, taking the smallest step backward in fear she'd be seen. She had known there were farms on the moors, but she'd been positive she was headed *away* from all traces of civilization.

  A pit of indecision opened in her stomach. Going forward would mean risking being seen by the farmer or farmhands but going back would mean facing another day of awful Hunger. Tears bubbled in the corners of her eyes, and she blinked them away, tipping her head up to stare at the bleak, empty sky.

  "I don't deserve this!" she screamed out at the nothingness. "I never deserved this life!"

  Shuffling sounds came from the shadows around the farmhouse, and she gasped, confident someone was staring at her. She ran in the opposite direction, keeping the river to her right. Heart thrumming in her ears, she lost sense of her surroundings and stopped running only when her knees gave out.

  The dead silence of the night surrounded her, and she let out the smallest sigh of relief. If she *had* been spotted, whoever it was hadn't followed her. Cora used the opportunity to catch her breath and plan her next move. The uneven ground split the water into two paths much thinner than the original, but they were still too wide for her to cross with her limited energy.

  Hugging the dead wolf to her chest, as if it were a child she was mourning, she followed the closest of the two streams for what felt like an eternity. In her state of disarray, it almost felt as if she were sleepwalking, her body separate from her consciousness. The ground ended suddenly, dropping a few feet below. Cora managed to stop before plummeting over the edge. Water cascaded down, and Cora did her best to see how far the drop was.

I don't know where I am.

She could've been uneasy, but instead, she took the unfamiliarity as a good sign. If nothing looked familiar, then she was truly in the wilderness. The *Fear Gorta* could be *anywhere*. Cora dropped to her hands and knees, getting as close as she could to the ground, trying to see to the bottom through the darkness. Her sight told her nothing, so she used her ears, listening to the way the water crashed below.

I can make it, she decided and swung her legs over the edge of the cliff.

On second thought, she grabbed the wolf and let herself fall, making sure it stayed between her and where she assumed the ground was as a makeshift cushion. The darkness gave the jump an ethereal feeling, as if she were jumping from one world to the next.

She landed with a thud, the breath whooshing out of her where the wolf pressed against her ribs. Her teeth slammed together, and her bag struck her shoulder with force, but other than that, she was unharmed. Dazed, she sat up and patted herself for injuries. Finding none, she stood up and surveyed her surroundings.

Bright neon green flashes, fireflies she realized, buzzed in the air, emanating enough light to see the canopy of branches overhead. On either side of her, the trees grew close together, so close it would be hard to try to go through them.

MEMENTO MORI

There's only one way forward.

A flash of green lit the air an inch from her nose, and she froze. The color pulled free all the memories she'd managed to suppress, and in her mind's eye, she could see the monster she had encountered.

The monster she most definitely *had* denied food.

Cora balled her hands into fists, craning her head back to see up the cliff she'd fallen from. *What was I thinking?* she asked herself on the verge of hyperventilating. *I can't do this. I can't beat that thing.*

She took a step away from the tunnel and toward the cliff when her foot hit the wolf's back.

You're capable of more than you think.

Cora closed her eyes, trying to get her breathing under control. She felt as if she were spiraling, like the world was moving too fast to process. If she simply laid down in the dirt, and let the hunger claim her, would anyone search for her?

Agnes would.

She'd be the first to notice and would know exactly what had happened.

What would happen to her if she came out this far?

Cora didn't want to picture it. Thinking of the elderly woman climbing down the steep cliff got her moving again. She scooped up the wolf and made her way down the seemingly endless trail of vines and trees. Several times, she glanced over her shoulder, worried she would lose sight of the way out.

Up ahead, the branches loosened, crafting a large archway that marked the beginning of a clearing. In the low light, the grass was a soft green highlighted by fragmented moonlight shining through the gaps. Bushes edged the clearing, along with black, unforgiving trees. Branches grew in a mesh far above her head, giving her the feeling that she was inside an actual building.

The darkness around the edges of the clearing somehow grew darker, the air harder to breathe. Cora feared she was on the verge of another panic attack when the shadows *moved*, gathering into one solid form on the other side of the clearing. She couldn't decipher the gap she'd squeezed through. The trees were a wall of foliage.

The ball of shadows started to take shape, the tentacles and almost human-like appendages, the same from her memories. A creature from her worst nightmares.

Cora froze. She'd come this far only to have no idea what to do when it mattered the most. Whether it be from fear or a reflex reaction, she threw the wolf carcass. It didn't go far, sitting in the grass between them as an odd sort of summary of all that had transpired in the past two days.

"I'm sorry!" Cora blurted out.

She had no idea if the thing could understand her or not, but she wanted to say her piece anyway. "I'm sorry I sent ye away when all ye wanted was food. I'm sorry I was selfish and didn't think about others. Others who have it worse than me. It's a cold, hard, world, and I never realized that in trying to survive, I'd become par' of it."

The beast opened and closed its mouth, fluttering its neon green tongue. It huffed, the sound reminding her of an angry horse, and Cora had the horrific image of it charging

MEMENTO MORI

toward her, the tentacles wrapping around her throat and squeezing the life from her.

She dropped to her knees and grabbed the wolf, shoving it forward a few more inches. "I know it isn't much, and it's far past due, but please, take this humble sacrifice. I- it's all I have."

The creature made no sound as it approached. It glided over the grass and stopped beside the wolf. Cora pulled away to put some space between them.

The tentacles on the beast's shoulders elongated, reminding her of a snake when they shot toward the ground. The ghastly appendages wrapped around the wolf's front and back legs, lifting it into the air. The mouth opened, stretching to consume the carcass whole. With a heavy *crunch*, the jaws shut. The Hungry One's eyes moved to her, and she dug her fingers into the grass until dirt wedged beneath her nails. She hadn't considered what might happen if it *didn't* accept her offer. The creature moved closer. She didn't move, afraid that if she did, the tentacles would be slung in her direction, and she'd be too caught off guard to react on time.

Cora met its glowing eyes, unable to break the connection. The green faded away, the edges of the clearing lost to darkness. Her eyes burned. The color returned, but her field of vision shrunk. Dizzy, she tilted her head before she crashed to the ground, the grass soft as it tickled her cheek.

Before the blackness claimed her, a voice rumbled through her mind that wasn't her own. *Thank you.*

KAYLA FREDERICK

MEMENTO MORI

In her life, she found the perfect death. A way to drown out the pain, a way to let go.

KAYLA FREDERICK

MEMENTO MORI

Dolls

1.

NATACHA BADEAU WAS the most unusual member of my senior class in high school. She was quiet, the type to walk with her gaze planted firmly on the floor as if it were whispering the secrets of life to her. Even while crossing the stage to get her diploma, when her eyes should've been up, focused on the path ahead, it was down on her feet.

I didn't expect her to show up for the ten-year reunion. She hadn't enjoyed her time in high school so why on God's green Earth would she ever show up for a tiny snapshot of it now? Not that I blamed her. I almost didn't go myself. I hadn't been that much farther up the social ladder than Natacha.

I made the decision to go only after my friend Madeline convinced me the reunion would be worth my time. That it would be good to *relive* the old days. I didn't agree but thought it might be fun to see how my classmates had fared after so many years.

Walking into the old gym that used to be filled with taunts and torments during PE class hits differently ten years down the road. It seems *smaller*, as if it had shrunken without us to fill it. Madeline flitted away from me nearly the minute we got there, chatting with old friends and running into their embrace as if no time had passed.

I stayed to myself, pouring a tiny paper cup of punch.

Madeline had been my only friend back then as she was now. Taking a tiny sip, I walked a lap around the gym, scouring the semi-familiar faces. Some people I could name like I'd seen them yesterday while others I would've never guessed I shared the same halls with for four years.

When Natacha walked in, there was no mistaking who she was. She was tall, her skin and eyes dark brown. Her black hair was hidden beneath a white scarf wrapped tightly over the top of her head. Her thin body was swathed in a loose-fitting gown of the same color. Natacha had never been shy about her Haitian heritage, but she'd never been outspoken about it either. After graduation, I'd heard rumors that Natacha had gone to live with her grandparents in Haiti for a few years. I don't know when she'd come back to town, but it felt oddly good to see her, my fellow outcast.

The gym, which only moments before had been loud with chatter, went silent. Natacha swept her gaze from one end of the room to the other but didn't step inside. I wondered if she still felt like an outsider all these years later. The air buzzed with so much history, so much tension, that it felt as if we were still in high school and the past ten years had been nothing but my imagination.

Except it wasn't. We were adults. Hell, some of us had children of our own, but I had a habit of wanting to see the best in people. Maybe that was foolish.

As our Prom Queen, Carly, soon proved. Her voice was the first to break the silence, and that was perhaps why it sounded so shrill, so harsh. "Come to spread a curse?" she jeered.

With the voice of their displeased leader in the air, others sprang to her side. "This is a *Christian* town," someone else called.

Then *everyone* started. For being religious people, they'd shifted to a rioting crowd of bigots awful fast.

Natacha took it all in without saying a word. Her head stayed high, face not changing expression. When her survey of the room came to an end she said, "You will all remember what you have done," and walked calmly out of the gym.

Raucous laughter followed her out, but I stayed silent. Dread crept down my spine, the warning bouncing around inside my head. The gym returned to the state it had been in before Natachu's appearance, but my nerves did not.

KAYLA FREDERICK

2.

I WANTED TO leave. I couldn't explain the feeling, but my skin crawled with it. The sensation of something bad looming in the near future engulfed me. I made a move for the door when Madeline caught me by the crook of the elbow.

"Are you leaving?" she asked.

"Yeah, I've got to open the bank in the morning," I said, reaching up to rub my eyes to exaggerate how tired I was.

"Boo. Stay a little longer. It's not every day your reunion comes around," she said, staring at me with her gigantic gray eyes.

Thankfully. I wanted to stick to my guns, but I melted under her gaze. "Fine, fine. Another hour, but that's it."

"Yay!" she said, clapping excitedly.

Then she promptly ditched me. In the arms of her on-again, off-again boyfriend, I was dust in the wind. I would've been angry, and I was, but it wasn't at her. It was at myself. I hadn't wanted to come to this to begin with, but I'd given in to make her happy.

I need spine, I chastised myself and started the long walk home alone.

I would give Madeline a thorough lashing in the morning. For now, I focused on getting home safe, not that I was particularly afraid. This town had been my home since I learned how to walk. I could've done this trip blindfolded if I wanted.

I took a detour through the park, trying to shave off every minute I could. The path led past the old picnic area. It was darker away from the street. A light sat at the start of the path and the end, but the middle crossed through a patch of trees and shadows.

I hurried through the stretch of darkness, stumbling over my feet. A rock rolled beneath my shoe, and I stumbled. Thankfully, the nearest tree was close enough to balance me without too much damage done. Gasping, I stood up straight, and that was when I saw it—a white figure hanging from the tree. It was the size of my palm, and I would've missed it if I hadn't nearly hit my head on it. I reached up, grazing my fingers over it. It was soft but steady, reminding me of a cat toy. Something designed for the sole purpose of being destroyed.

I let it go and looked into the branches. Dozens of dolls hung from strings around their necks. My eyes darted from one to another. Some of them had been colored with different splotches of red, black, and yellow.

"What the hell is this?" I asked and took a step backward, away from them.

All I could think of were voodoo dolls.

They would like Natacha for this. After what had happened at the reunion, she didn't need a gruesome prank hanging over her head.

I can't let anyone see these, I decided.

I'd never done anything in the past to save her. I'd seen the bullying firsthand, but out of fear for myself, I'd looked the other way.

I didn't have to be that person anymore.

With shaking fingers, I reached into my pocket for my knife. A few slashes, and a few minutes later, all the dolls laid scattered on the ground. I bundled as many as I could in my arms, vowing to come back for the rest as soon as I could. I glanced

KAYLA FREDERICK

around, making sure no one noticed, before I hurried home to toss them into the bottom of my closet.

MEMENTO MORI

3.

I WENT BACK for the rest of the dolls, and by the time I made it back home, I was so tired, I fell right to sleep. When I woke a few hours later, it was thanks to the sound of a firetruck blazing down the street. I jumped out of bed before my eyes were open all the way. Struggling with the blinds, I peered outside. Through the flashing red and blue lights, the flicker of red-orange flames became apparent.

That was Carly's house.

I hurried outside and joined the group of people converged on the street. They were loading someone onto an ambulance. I didn't have to see the stretcher to know it was our Prom Queen, fallen from glory.

My stomach sloshed, and I had the fear I would vomit right there in the street for everyone to see. Hand over my mouth, I hurried back inside in time to lose my stomach contents into the toilet. I sat on the bathroom floor, staring at the wall, and thinking of the dolls, particularly the one that had been colored black. It wasn't possible that *Natacha* had something to do with what had happened to Carly, was it?

I tried to tell myself to get ready for work, but when I opened my closet, I could see the doll.

You're being crazy, I told myself. *It was an accident. Accidents happen.*

I would call down to the hospital later and see if Carly was okay. For now, I had to start my day. I showered and pulled my hair into its usual ponytail before slipping into my pantsuit.

KAYLA FREDERICK

My head hurt, and I didn't feel great, but at least my face showed no signs of my internal turmoil. The drive to work was easy, but when I got there, I nearly plowed into a curb looking at the caution tape strewn across the front of the building. Shattered glass was sprayed over the stairs, and I hurried to find a safe place to park so I could get answers. Three cop cars sat in the street, the red and blue lights illuminating a body being loaded into an ambulance. I struggled to process what I was seeing.

How could this town oversee two tragedies in the span of a few hours? It was unthinkable.

I hurried up to the nearest officer who stood halfway between his car and the broken window, talking into a walkie talkie.

"Ma'am, you need to take a step back," he said as soon as he spotted me.

"My name is Harley. I was supposed to work first shift today. Please tell me what's happened."

He reached up to take off his hat before scratching the top of his head. "I can't say too much right now, but it seems someone's broken in. Taken some money and valuables."

"Was anyone hurt?" I demanded, thinking of my boss, Jason. It was odd to think of him that way, if I was being honest. He was the same age as me, but he'd gotten himself in the workforce years before me and worked his way up to branch manager. When I'd come in desperate for a job, he'd hired me on the spot simply because he remembered me from high school.

The officer dropped his gaze, and a sickening feeling washed through my gut.

"I can't say right now," he said.

MEMENTO MORI

But he didn't have to. The feeling in my gut spoke for me.

"Thank you," I told him and rushed to the payphone at the bus stop across the street, dropping in all the quarters I could dig out of my pocket. "Operator, connect me to Lakeview Hospital."

I waited a minute as I was connected with a receptionist. "Hello, Lakeview Hospital."

"Hi, yeah. My name is Harley. There was a patient admitted early this morning. Carly Hughes. She was in a fire. I…I need to know if she's okay."

The receptionist was quiet for a long minute before she said, "Ma'am, I can't give out personal details over the phone."

That was all I needed to hear to know that she was dead and so was Jason.

I had no memory of going home. The next time I came to, I was dropping to my knees on the floor of my bedroom, digging through the dolls. I pulled out the one that had been colored black and flipped it over. In the back was a slit. I stuck my fingers into it. Something sharp poked me.

"Ouch!" I exclaimed and carefully dug it out. It was a folded piece of cardstock.

Carly Hughes, had been written inside.

I wanted to puke again. I dug through the rest of the dolls, pulling out the name cards before finding Jason's. It was void of any color except for one splash of red over the place where its head would've been.

"No," I whispered, dropping them to the floor.

I went through the rest, paying attention to the red and black scores, and most importantly, the spots where there were no colors at all. Every doll had something in the way of a damning mark, and that sense of foreboding, of dread, rose until I thought it would choke me.

Then I found mine with a red slash across the throat.

MEMENTO MORI

4.

I DIDN'T KNOW what to do. What I *could* do. Who would believe me when I said *voodoo dolls* had burned down Carly's house and robbed the bank? There was only one person I could talk to, and I wondered how that would go. I had never considered Natacha to be an enemy like so many of our classmates did, but we weren't friends either. In high school, the only difference between me and her was pure luck. I thought of all the bullying I'd seen and walked away from and guilt settled in my stomach. I'd never been brave enough to step in.

You made your choice.

I thought of my doll. It seemed as if Natacha had made her choice too.

Unsure what to do, I wandered back to the park in the oncoming night, to the spot where I had found the dolls. The strings were still there, blowing in the breeze. With uncertain fingers, I reached up, touching the shredded ends. I didn't know what I expected to find, but it wasn't here. I was ready to go home when scuffling from the trees caught my attention. I squinted, trying to see what lurked in the darkness.

"Hello?"

Two glowing eyes peered back. My jaw opened for a scream, but no sound came out. I took a hurried step back, nearly falling over myself to get away.

"Harley," a voice greeted me.

Natacha took one step out of the trees, detaching from the shadows. "What are you doing here?"

"I could ask you the same," I said, wanting to have strength and conviction in my voice, but I could barely hear myself. I was *afraid*. Before the reunion, I'd never heard her speak. After everything that had happened, everything I suspected her of, it sent chills down my spine.

"You took my dolls," she said, voice stiff. Cold. Accusatory.

"Yes," I said. "Why? Why did…you do those things to Carly and Jason?"

"Why do you assume I'm to blame?"

"The incident at the reunion…"

"Shows what kind of people *they* are," Natacha replied. "Not me."

"But the dolls are yours. They…" I trailed off, angry that I couldn't seem to find the words to finish my sentences.

"They harvest their own energy," she said. "I merely created them. When you cut the strings, you unleashed their power."

"Why did you leave them here where anyone could find them?"

"It's poetic justice for this town to destroy itself. So many Christians in this place are filled with such hypocrisy. A town like this deserves torment. Call it a cleansing if you will."

"I agree that a lot of people are shitty, but violence is never the answer."

"I assume you found *your* doll."

I drew my eyebrows together, wanting to demand how she knew, but I composed myself and said, "I'm not like them."

"Aren't you though? You stood by and let it happen,

MEMENTO MORI

fearful only of what would happen to yourself. You are guilty by association."

Lip twitching, I doubled my hands into fists, wishing I could argue, but I had no grounds to do so. She was right. "So don't stoop to their level. You have to fix this."

"What's done is done," she said. "I suggest you leave town. Forget what's happened here and start your life anew."

"And if I refuse?"

"Karma will find you too."

KAYLA FREDERICK

5.

THAT NIGHT, I stayed at the library as long as the librarian would allow, learning all I could about Vodou culture and religion. They have good Gods and bad spirits called loas. Really, it wasn't so different from any other religion. It was television, movies, *Hollywood* that distorted the reality of an entire culture.

What Natacha was doing wasn't traditional Vodou. From what I had gathered, she was a *caplata*, a type of witch who could use the loas for good or evil. That meant I had no idea if Natacha was lying about her curse, and how I could break it if she wasn't.

Leave town, her words echoed in my head.

When I was kicked from the library, I tried to go home and sleep, but it became impossible. Every time I closed my eyes, the image of the beast in the shadows came to me. Its mouth full of sharp teeth that could slice through flesh so it could lick up the blood.

Over the course of the next seventy-two hours, classmate after classmate succumbed to tragedy. In my room, I sorted through the pile of dolls, trying to keep track of the ones who had been hurt or killed. The smaller that pile grew, the more my dread rose. I couldn't save any of them, and I had tried. While predicting what fate would come to who was growing easier, determining who would feel Natacha's wrath next was impossible.

The pile whittled down to two dolls, Madeline and myself.

From the day of the reunion, I hadn't spoken a word to her. She'd called several times to apologize for ditching me, but I hadn't answered. She most likely thought I was still angry at her, but the reality was that in the wake of all I had learned about Natacha, none of that mattered.

Until now.

For the first time since this had begun, I picked up the phone, ringing Madeline. I expected her to answer right away so when she didn't, I felt sick with the certainty that she was in danger.

I didn't think about what I *could* or *should* do next. I hurried out to my car, driving as fast as I could to her house. I didn't wonder which of the two of us would be the loas' next target. When I rounded onto her block, I could see her headlights as she backed down her driveway.

"No, no, no," I choked, flooring it to make the car go a little bit faster.

I tried to block her from pulling into the street, but it didn't work. Madeline eased around me and continued on to wherever it was that she was going. I had no choice but to follow. When she stopped, I'd tell her what was going on.

It's going to be okay, I tried to tell myself.

Then she turned onto the highway leading out of town. Alarm bells rang inside my head, warning me not to follow, but how could I listen? I raced after her, staying two lanes over.

You stood by and let it happen, fearful only of what would happen to yourself. Natacha's voice bounced around my head.

That's not me anymore, I thought back.

I was determined to save Madeline and put an end to this. As if that thought was the trigger, my worst fear came true. The car ahead of me swerved, trying to avoid crashing into a car that had gone sideways in the lane. It didn't work. Metal crunched and screeched as cars mashed together. I stomped on the brake, trying to get my car to stop before it joined the pile.

No such luck.

It skidded forward, spinning one-eighty from the force of the brake. Madeline's blue sedan appeared a second before I propelled into it. My body jostled from the impact, every bone in my body aching, and I grasped the steering wheel, prepared for the airbag that never deployed. Glass shattered and metal crunched, the world around me a spiral of colors and movement. Then the car righted itself and stopped moving. Blood poured down my temple from a cut on my forehead. The smell of gas filled my nostrils, but I didn't know if it came from my car or one of the others nearby.

Shaking, I undid the seatbelt, barely missing the sharp jagged piece of glass embedded in the seat beside me. It had been meant *for* me, I was sure of it when I remembered the single gash on my doll's throat.

I can't beat it, I decided, peering into the crushed remains of Madeline's car.

Her doll had been splattered with red, a great many injuries all at once. The doll had confused me, but it made sense now. No one in that car could've lived through the wreckage. The accident had been a means of taking us *both* out, but somehow, I was lucky. If the airbag had deployed, I would've been sent backward into the glass shard and killed.

By the mere grace of God, I'd escaped Death's clutches. In my head, a clock started to tick down. If I didn't take myself out of the game, the game would take me out of it. Natacha had done me a kindness that she hadn't shown anyone else. She'd given me a head start, a chance, and I'd be a fool to ignore it.

Blood dotted my shirt, and I didn't know how many injuries I had, but with my flood of adrenaline, nothing hurt. I opened the door, trotting away from the crash. My legs were like noodles, and I fell to my hands and knees, nearly dragging myself across the concrete to the city limits.

When I crossed the line, Madeline's car exploded, catching the rest of the pile in a great blaze that rose into the sky. I rested my cheek to the cool concrete and cried.

KAYLA FREDERICK

MEMENTO MORI

Of course, history has a way of repeating itself. Rather than learning from the mistakes of people past, we find ourselves making the same decisions and hoping for a different outcome—true insanity.

KAYLA FREDERICK

Footsteps

1.

HANDS HELD OUT before her, Fiona took in a deep breath and closed her eyes. The smell of incense went deep into her lungs, and she let her eyes flutter open. In the dim light seeping under the flaps of her tent, she made out details of the things around her. A table with a crystal ball. A trunk in the corner that was empty, only situated there for ambiance. On the other side of the table sat a young woman. She wiped her eyes with a napkin, clutching the white fabric tight between dabs.

"I guess if I could ask her anything, I'd want to be sure that she's at peace," she said.

Fiona bobbed her head but kept her hands lifted above the crystal ball. She gazed into it, pretending to see something in its depths.

"Tell her I am. Tell her not to mourn too much for me," the elderly woman in the corner of the room said.

Fiona kept her eyes on the crystal ball though she wanted to look to the woman instead. She was dead, but Fiona still felt it rude to not acknowledge her as she spoke.

"She says she's somewhere safe. She doesn't want you to lose yourself in mourning for her and wants you to live a long, happy life," Fiona said, leaning closer to the ball.

The girl dabbed her face again, smiling through the tears.

KAYLA FREDERICK

The red streaks gave her an ethereal beauty that she hadn't had when she'd first arrived. She reached one dainty hand across the table and grasped Fiona's before she stood up.

"Thank you for this," she said, tossing a neatly folded ten-dollar bill on the table and leaving the tent.

Fiona sat back in her seat and grabbed the money, tucking it away into the pocket in her robes. Not a bad tip for ten minutes. Relieved for the break, she sat back in her seat and slipped a cigarette from the pack, taking a puff before looking at the elderly woman in the corner.

"Thank you for your counsel," she told her.

The elderly woman vanished in a spray of mist. Fiona closed her eyes and took another drag of her cigarette, opening them again to watch the smoke tendrils rise, mixing with the heavy haze of incense.

A pit of *something* sat in her stomach. A feeling she couldn't identify. Many people considered mediums to be frauds, but what she was doing was a good thing. She gave people closure. Not like the "palm reader" a few tents down. She was nothing short of a scam artist.

If Fiona ever lost her gift, it would be the end of her business, and she'd be fine with that. She didn't really do what she did for the money, which was good since it didn't pay that much anyway. No, she did it for the feeling that coursed through her now. The feeling that she was doing the one thing she'd been put on Earth to achieve.

There had been a time in her life when she hadn't believed in ghosts, hadn't believed there was *anything* on the other side. That was years ago, and Fiona could hardly remember that version of herself. She watched the glowing orange tip of the cigarette before she snubbed it out and tossed the butt to the floor. They didn't really want any of the workers smoking in their tents, but they also didn't have a way to enforce that. Fiona knew she wasn't the only one to sneak one between customers. Ally, the fake palm reader girl, was usually slinking around smoking *something*. Most of the time, it wasn't cigarettes.

A loud whoosh filled the room, the candles on the table beside the antique chest flickering, threatening to go out. Fiona froze. Not out of fear, but out of familiarity. This was a ghost she'd seen often. One much more powerful than the usual spirits she dealt with on a day-to-day basis. In all truthfulness, she wasn't sure *what* he was, but she was grateful for his visits since he often warned her of trouble to come.

Trouble was what had brought them together to begin with. That had been in her normal days, before everything had changed. She'd been driving down the street, the pounding rain on the windshield making it nearly impossible to see anything outside. She was going under the speed limit, but with her limited view of the road, it still felt too fast. The merge onto the highway was coming up, but she only she knew that from previous trips.

As she turned her car toward the on ramp, a soft voice whispered, *Stop now.*

She didn't know what made her obey, but she stomped on the brake, her car fishtailing as it tried to gain traction on the slippery cement. Before she merged onto the road that connected to the on-ramp, a speeding eighteen-wheeler roared past. Fiona sat behind the wheel, staring straight ahead in a mix of shock and fear. If she hadn't hit the brake, she would've been hit straight on.

KAYLA FREDERICK

She would be dead.

Over the course of the next few months, she'd learned the truth about the voice that had saved her. It belonged to a guardian deity. While she saw many ghosts, none of them came back to see her after she helped them move on. He was the only one she saw regularly. She didn't know much about him, other than what he looked like—thin and pale with wispy black hair and piercing brown eyes.

Beside that first encounter, they usually only spoke through dreams. For him to be *here*, when she was awake, must mean her life was in danger again. She shifted her gaze from her discarded cigarette butt to his faded outline in the corner of the tent. His eyes were the clearest part of him as if he wanted to make sure she really saw him. Maybe more importantly, he wanted to make sure *he* saw *her*.

"It's been a while," she said at last, breaking the heavy silence.

"It has. You've been doing much better in life," he said, the words echoing out of him from some place in his abdomen.

"But something's about to happen, isn't it? That's why you're here."

"Someone bad is lurking in this town," he confirmed. "And I fear that he may cross paths with you."

Fiona drew her eyebrows together. "Who is it?"

"I don't know, and that is the problem."

Fiona rose to her feet. "Wait, how can you know they're a threat if you don't know who they are?"

"Whoever they are, the very nearness of their soul, their aura, has been enough to tip the balance of energy in this town.

MEMENTO MORI

There's darkness here, driven by forces more powerful than the normal human can obtain."

"Are you saying that they're possessed?"

"That may be the case," he said. "Or they may simply be filled with a kind of evil I've never come across before. Whatever the case, they will sense your power, and they will come for you."

Fiona balled her hand into a fist and set it to the table, thinking. She'd never known this deity to lie. He had no reason to, but if he didn't know things, how in the world could she hope to figure them out?

"So what should I—" She started but stopped abruptly when she realized he was gone.

2.

FIONA SPENT THE rest of the day wary of every customer who came into her tent. In her downtime, she stared hatefully at the crystal ball on her table. Why couldn't it actually tell her the future rather than be a fancy prop? She passed the time by summoning a few ghosts, interrogating them the best she could, but none of them knew more than her guardian did.

Fiona felt secluded in her concerns, her fears. If only Ally wasn't a phony. For a moment, she sat with her face buried in her hands. Her body itched with the desire to get up, to move. Maybe a walk would get her brain working properly.

On the way out of the tent, she grabbed her *Be Back Soon* sign and slapped it onto the patch of Velcro on the front of her tent. The fairgrounds smelled of sweets and fried food. Dozens of voices rose up around her, crowds filled with people from old to young. As patiently as she could, she made her way through them, dodging the trash that some people had been too lazy to throw away on their own. Sighing, she bent down to scoop up the discarded cup and wrappers and made her way to the nearest trash can. It was overflowing with similar wrappers, but Fiona did what she could to put the garbage where it belonged.

She stopped, suddenly aware of how *wrong* the air felt. It was like the deity had said, the energy had changed. The air still smelt the same, but a feeling of vulnerability gave her chills. She wrapped her arms around herself, trying to block out the unmistakable feeling of being watched.

A scream rang out from a few tents down, *Ally's* tent, and

MEMENTO MORI

Fiona froze the way she had the day she'd watched that truck barrel less than two feet past the front of her car. A few people rushed toward the sound, but most of them waited to see the drama unfold. Fiona fought her way through the crowd.

The first person who had gone inside came out and bent over, hurling into the grass. A minute later, someone else stumbled out and yelled, "Someone call 911!"

This was what Fiona had been warned about, wasn't it?

The crowd started to move. Some people away from the scene, and others toward it. A few stopped to fumble for their phones and call for help. Fiona pushed ahead until the red and white flaps of the palm reader's tent loomed before her. She made her way inside, expecting to see that the girl had collapsed, a fainting spell from the heat.

The inside of the tent was a lot like Fiona's with the haze of incense, odd but useless decorations, and the table in the middle. The major difference? The enormous blood splatters. Ally was stretched out in the grass beside her table, eyes staring straight ahead. Blood covered the bottom half of her face and her chest from the massive gash across her throat.

The scent of blood filled Fiona's nose, and the world went sideways before cutting to black.

KAYLA FREDERICK

3.

WHEN FIONA OPENED her eyes, the ceiling above her was white, and for a second, she was confused. Then she remembered what had happened. The blood inside the tent, the scene of Ally's body, and then the overwhelming smell that had hit her. The EMT beside her raised an eyebrow in concern.

"What do you remember?" she asked as Fiona pulled herself into a sitting position.

"Ally," she said softly, and hated that her name was enough to bring the cascade of gruesome images back to the front of her mind.

The EMT dabbed Fiona's head with a cool rag before she set it to the side. Fiona looked around and realized she was in the back of an ambulance parked in the middle of the fairgrounds.

"You fainted," she said, observing Fiona's knitted brow. "After what was in that tent, I can't say I blame you."

Ally's bloody body came to the front of her mind again, and Fiona looked for an escape. According to her guardian deity, something like this had been bound to happen. Could it be that the killer hadn't meant to harm Ally but had been after *her* instead?

Shivering, Fiona climbed out of the ambulance. The EMT called after her, but she wasn't in the mood to listen. As soon as her feet touched down on the grass, she stopped to watch two coroners carrying a stretcher between them. A white sheet was draped over the top, but there was no mistaking what it was hiding. Blood soaked through in a few places, and to Fiona, she could see the body as clearly as if they hadn't bothered to cover her up at all.

    Fiona turned away, bowing her head in respect. She would see Ally again, and when she did, she'd ask her how she came to this unfortunate end.

KAYLA FREDERICK

4.

FIONA WASN'T SURPRISED when their manager decided to close the fair that night and send everyone home. In fact, she was *relieved*. This was the perfect opportunity for her to plan out what she   should do, while distraction free. The drive home, she was so lost in her thoughts that she was surprised she didn't get into a wreck. A few times, she questioned if the green lights she'd gone through had really been green.

Once she was safely home, she changed out of her robes, the unmistakable smell of coppery blood still clinging to them, and put on a sweatshirt and jogging pants instead. She brewed a cup of tea, hoping it would settle her stomach, but her insides still rioted with nausea. She never had been able to stand the sight, or *smell*, of blood. Every time she closed her eyes, she could see the scene again. It hadn't been a murder.

It had been a *massacre*.

Fiona tried to imagine other scenarios that could lead to such an ending. Could other people have figured out that Ally was a fraud? Could they have been so angered by the deception that they would want to harm her? It seemed petty, but to Fiona, a lot of human nature was. People had been killed for much less.

She set her cup down onto her coffee table with a soft thud. She'd barely had more than a few sips, but it was enough. With a glance at the square clock on the wall, she calculated the time that had passed. Ally was most likely tucked away into her own little freezer drawer in the morgue by now.

Rising to her feet, Fiona grabbed her keys and went out

MEMENTO MORI

the door.

5.

THE FAIR WAS eerie when the sun went down. Bathed in the darkness of night and void of all humans, it was worse than in the daytime. Fiona hugged herself as she walked between the tents. It was all too easy to imagine eyes peering at her from every shadow. A few times, she wondered if it was all in her head or if the killer was still lurking the grounds, waiting for someone like her to stumble into his path.

She reached for the handle of the butcher knife she'd slipped into the waistband of her pants. Coming out here without a weapon seemed like a foolish idea. Since she didn't own a taser or pepper spray, she was limited to what her kitchen had to offer.

As soon as Ally's tent appeared, something tightened in Fiona's chest. They hadn't been close, but fair folk were like family, and it was odd to think they'd lost one of their own. They'd spent so much time around one another since the summer began that opening in the morning without her seemed wrong.

Caution tape looped across the entrance of Ally's tent. One strand had come loose and crinkled in the soft breeze.

Fiona watched it and pushed out her senses, trying to pick up a trace of Ally in the Veil that separated this world from the next. She took a breath and tried again, but there was no trace of her. Fiona pushed away her reservations and ducked under the caution tape. Inside the tent, the smell was worse than it had been earlier. She leaned against the wall, trying to compose herself.

Don't pass out, she told herself, taking in deep breaths through her mouth. It didn't help.

MEMENTO MORI

Sniffling, she took two steps in, looking around. It was dark, and Fiona fumbled to pull a lighter from her pocket. In the low light, she could see dark stains. Careful not to step in any of them, she crouched down beside the spot where Ally had lain in her final moments. Fiona closed her eyes, trying again to pierce through the Veil. There was nothing but darkness and a cold that seeped deep down to Fiona's bones.

The girl wasn't here.

In the case of violent deaths, the spirits usually stayed close to the scene. Most of the time, they didn't know they were dead, but Ally was gone.

Maybe she stayed with her body.

It was much rarer but not unheard of. Fiona had the image of Ally being stuffed into one of those tiny silver freezers and imagined her spirit standing outside, trying to find a way to open the door and get to herself.

That was certainly no afterlife anyone should ever experience.

To the morgue I go.

KAYLA FREDERICK

6.

SITTING IN THE hospital parking lot, Fiona was hesitant to get out of the car. This close to the morgue, she felt uneasy and it would get worse the closer she got. Connecting to any spirit for a length of time was trying when it was one-on-one. In the morgue, there was no telling how many spirits lurked, desperate to reach out and connect with her, the only person who could see them. She wished she could help them all, but if the deity was right, she had bigger things to worry about.

Finding Ally's spirit was the only way for her to get some answers. She kept that thought at the front of her mind as she climbed out of the car. Her footsteps seemed unusually loud as she crossed the parking lot. She felt small and vulnerable, and the paranoid feeling of being watched had followed her here.

The electric sliding door opened with a whoosh, spilling cool air-conditioned air into her face. It felt good. Until then, she hadn't realized how much she had sweat, and regretted her choice of clothes. As soon as she surveyed her surroundings, she had no idea how she could hope to pull this off. There would most likely be checks in place to keep random people from wandering into the morgue. Not to mention the woman sitting behind the reception desk, glaring at her. One hand remained hidden on her lap, and Fiona could imagine it hovered near a panic button.

"What can I do for you, ma'am?" she asked.

Fiona opened her mouth, but no words came out. She couldn't lie and say she was visiting someone. The giant sign next to the receptionist with the visitor hours crossed that avenue off

MEMENTO MORI

for her.

    A hazy image of a girl appeared beside the receptionist. When Fiona blinked, the apparition was gone, and the woman was asleep. Fiona didn't move, unsure what to do. A few times, she'd seen ghosts able to move objects, sometimes whisper to people who were still alive, but she'd never seen them able to do more than that. The hazy apparition appeared again, closer. The white edges of the being flickered as if she were ready to disappear from existence entirely. The white incorporeal form shifted into a familiar face.

    Ally. A deep sadness haunted her eyes so profoundly that death couldn't erase it. "You came to find out the truth," she said.

    "Who did this to you?"

    "I don't...know," Ally replied, words rising and lowering in pitch as if her voice were coming through a radio and the signal wasn't good.

    "Was it someone we've seen before?"

    "No," Ally said. For a solid minute, she disappeared, and Fiona thought that was it. That she was done talking to her. When she came back, the sadness was stronger. "Whatever it is, he feeds on energy, Fiona. Every ounce. It doesn't stop at death."

    As if to punctuate her point, she vanished again. Fiona waited, expecting her to come back, but she never did.

KAYLA FREDERICK

7.

DESPITE THE SUMMER heat, the trip home through the suburban neighborhoods left Fiona cold. As cold as the blast of air from the hospital lobby. She thought of death, and that made her think of Ally. Perhaps the only thing worse than dying was to die a *second* death.

Could that be possible?

If Ally was right, if whoever had killed her was feeding on her energy, what did that make him? Some kind of energy vampire? The more Fiona pondered, the more she realized she didn't know much about the other side. She knew how to deal with ghosts. That was easy. It was like talking to other humans. When it came to darker entities such as poltergeists, demons, and everything in between, she was clueless.

The idea of someone out there who was feeding on energy made her shiver. The fact the killer had targeted Ally, someone with a supposed connection to the other side, made it more interesting. Was that the energy he needed? An entity who needed psychic energy to survive? If that was the case, he would've been angry after killing Ally and finding out she possessed none of it.

You'd be next on his list.

Not only was Fiona the only other "medium" at the fair, but she was the only one in town who was legitimate.

As far as she knew.

I need to do my research.

MEMENTO MORI

8.

WHEN FIONA MADE it home, it was already well past her usual bedtime. Her eyelids drooped and her body yearned for sleep, but her mind was in hyperspeed, pumping her full of questions as a way of staving off the exhaustion. She brewed a pot of coffee, swigging down half her mug almost as soon as it was ready. Wincing at the pain in her scalded tongue, she sat down in front of her computer. She wasn't exactly sure how to go about getting the information she was after, but started to type anyway.

Clearview mediums, she wrote. She hated that her hometown had such a bland, generic name. How many towns in the country had a similar name? Hundreds of search results popped up. The first few weren't for her town so she narrowed it down by adding in her state.

Not much better.

An obituary popped up, and at first, Fiona thought that was the computer's way of being funny. *Why talk to ghosts when you can be one?* She rolled her eyes at her own brain as she clicked on it. Then she realized that it was an obituary for a medium in her town.

Madame Griselda.

The name sounded vaguely familiar. She'd had Fiona's job long before she did. Fiona squinted at the date of her death. According to this, Madame Griselda had died around the same time Fiona had acquired her powers.

She slumped against her seat, staring at the black and white image of the woman. In it, she was smiling, casting a playful look to whoever had taken the picture. She was much younger than the age the writing beside it said she'd been when she died. Fiona stared into her eyes. Could it be that the reason that Fiona had acquired her powers was because this woman had no longer needed hers?

Fiona pushed her chair away from the computer desk and rose to her feet. The event with Ally's ghost had taken about seventy percent of her energy, but Fiona was determined to use what was left to summon her guardian. He had to know if there was some kind of connection between her and Madame Griselda, right?

It couldn't be a coincidence.

Fiona squeezed her eyes shut until the pressure hurt. Over and over, she chanted, using everything she could think of to make him appear. On ordinary ghosts, this kind of thing worked. For him? It did not. She sat there, forcing herself to keep her eyes closed, but no familiar *whoosh* of cold wind announced his arrival, and she gave up. When she opened her eyes again, it was to stare at the grainy black and white image of Madame Griselda.

9.

FIONA WAS SO tired it took an exaggerated amount of effort to lay down in bed. Her jogging outfit had been suffocating outside, but in the cool air conditioning in her room, it was perfect.

When she opened her eyes, she was in a gray room. Golden sconces lined the wall, the flickering firelight the only bit of light around her. She did a full twirl before she came face to face with her guardian deity. His form was more solid when he appeared in her dreams. Those piercing eyes were still the most dominating feature.

"You knew Madame Griselda, didn't you?" she asked, figuring he already knew what she wanted to ask.

"I was...acquainted with her for a long time."

"What happened to her?" Fiona asked, thinking of the obituary. It had simply said she'd passed away. No details. Not much information at all, really.

"Madame Griselda fought for a long time against the forces on the other side of the Veil," the entity said. "Unfortunately, her human body couldn't withstand such a thing forever."

"You're saying she died of old age?" Fiona asked, surprised. She'd been certain that Miss Griselda had met the same sort of fate Ally had. The same fate Fiona would face if she didn't figure out how to stop the killer.

"She did. I was there to guide her to the Other Side."

Fiona considered what that meant. "Is there any way for me to contact her?"

The deity shook his head. "Even I cannot reach her now."

Fiona thought about that before she asked, "What exactly was it that she could do? Was she like me or was she...*different?*"

"Not only could she communicate with the dead, but she could control them. A reverse possession of sorts."

Fiona tried to think about what it would be like to jump *inside* of a ghost. "That sounds...eerie," she said, almost glad that she couldn't do it. "I guess what I'm really trying to find out is if I got her powers. Is that possible?"

Another flicker of that strange emotion that Fiona considered to be sadness crossed his face.

Fiona understood what it meant. "You brought me her powers, didn't you?"

His eyes softened to an emotion Fiona could no longer identify.

"Why?" she whispered.

"I cannot describe the exact trait that makes some humans prone to the delicacy of the Veil and the creatures on the other side. Madame Griselda had it, and you do too. When she passed, it left an opening in this town, one that could not be left unguarded."

"You're saying she protected us?" Fiona asked, then it clicked. "The creature, whatever it is, was something Madame Griselda kept at bay, wasn't it? Now that she's gone, it's seizing the opportunity to come through."

"It is a powerful creature. One that took much of Madame Griselda's energy to contain. Now that it's absorbed some life energy, I fear the damage it may be capable of."

MEMENTO MORI

10.

SOFT MORNING SUNLIGHT streamed in through the window on the other side of Fiona's room, but she turned her back to it, staring at the end table and lamp instead. She'd been perfectly fine with her gift when she imagined her entire purpose in life was helping restless spirits move on. To find out her *real* job was to keep evil spirits from crossing into their world was a new level of crazy she wasn't sure she could accept.

She was no protector. How in the world could she be expected to keep this entire town safe when she hadn't been able to save the girl who worked three tents down from her?

As she lay there with the sunbeam inching closer and closer to the bed, she started to wonder if maybe she *had* died the day she'd nearly avoided the semi. Maybe she hadn't been so fortunate and had been crushed beneath the wheels, ground into the grating, and smeared across the road.

Maybe all of this was her own afterlife and that was why she could speak to other ghosts. She was trapped in a loop of her own inability to move on.

Wouldn't that be some irony?

Eventually, her hip started to hurt so she flipped onto her back, staring up at the ceiling. Without much enthusiasm, she lifted her arm, pinching a chunk of skin. It turned red, a shoot of pain flooding through her. She didn't know if she should feel relieved or not. Could ghosts feel pain?

She had no idea.

Next time I meet one, that's the first thing I'm going to ask, she decided.

That made her think of work, and she glanced at the clock on her nightstand. It was already well past noon, and on a usual day, she had work around two. But this *wasn't* a normal day. This was the day after Ally's brutal demise. The tent was still technically a crime scene. One the police would never find evidence in if a demon really was responsible for her massacre. Fiona wondered if the fair would be open. A quick search on the computer confirmed it was.

When she closed out the window, the tab from last night came into view, Miss Griselda staring at her. Fiona shivered at the idea of the woman knowing about her long before Fiona had known about her. She hurried to close the window, not wanting to see her again.

A sense of paranoia washed over her as she went to work peeling off her dirty jogging outfit and changing into her robes and flowy "medium" costume. Fiona made her way to work, disappointed to hear cheerful voices and see smiling faces. Someone had died here, but for everyone else, life simply went on, no differently than it had been the day before.

On her way to her tent, Fiona waved to a few of the carnies that she passed, but only half of them bothered to return the gesture. They were mourning Ally's loss in their own way.

For the most part, things appeared the way they always did, outside *and* inside her tent, but it all felt different. Yesterday, her path in life had seemed so simple.

Today, it did not.

Fiona sank into her familiar padded chair, wrapping her hands around the arm rests. It would be hard to think of the mundane day ahead of her, the *normal* day, but she did her best to put herself into the mindset of the person she'd been twenty-four hours before. Fiona breathed out and let her eyes open. When they did, they landed on the crystal ball, and she had another moment of loathing for the prop.

Pointless.

Before she could look away, a haze formed inside it. She moved closer, nearly pressing her face to the smooth surface to see the swirling darkness inside. What was happening? She'd never seen images in it before. Until this moment, she'd assumed that people who claimed to see things in crystal balls were frauds. The smoke swirled and moved, a raging storm. It darkened and took a vaguely humanoid shape. Fiona furrowed her brow, trying to decide what it was.

Eyes the color of Ally's blood appeared, pressed to the glass from the other side. Fiona screamed and stumbled backward. Her foot caught the leg of her favorite chair, and she windmilled to keep herself from falling. In the commotion, her hand smacked the crystal ball off its cradle and onto the floor with a *crack*. Fiona caught her balance at the same time a man burst into the tent.

"Is everything okay? I heard someone yell," he said, scanning the room behind her as if he expected there to be another person.

Hesitantly, Fiona studied him. He wore a security outfit complete with mace, a flashlight, and a walkie-talkie hanging from his belt. He wasn't a security guard she *recognized*, but in light of yesterday's circumstances, it made sense that the fair would want to up their security presence. After all, who would want to go somewhere they could possibly be murdered?

Fiona's eyes lingered on the remaining shards of her crystal ball before she did her best to plaster a smile on her face. *Normal...you have to look normal,* she told herself.

"Yeah, I'm okay," she said. "I thought I saw a mouse."

The security guard's hardened face softened with relief. "We *are* outside."

"Yeah, I know. It was just unexpected," she said, thinking of the red eyes with a barely repressed shudder. She *wished* all she'd seen was a mouse. "Thank you for checking on me so quickly."

The warmth vanished from his face as Fiona went to work picking up glass shards. "We can't be too careful."

She said nothing, hoping that would end the conversation, but the man stayed by the door, watching her. He'd been nothing but nice, but she wished he would leave so she could sort what she had seen. Or *thought* she had seen.

"Well, if you need anything, I'll be doing my rounds around the booths," he said finally.

Fiona didn't look up until the swish of the tent flaps announced she was alone. She stared at the glass shards in her hand, imagining red eyes glaring out of each one. She'd never felt such evil before and hoped to never feel it again. Silently, she commended Madame Griselda for her dedication to the cause. Wrestling with literal demons every day?

That couldn't have been easy.

Fiona dumped the shards into the trashcan in the corner, listening to the tiny clanks against the plastic. Without the main adornment, her table seemed bare. She sat in the seat, staring at the empty cradle where the ball had sat.

MEMENTO MORI

Weak. She felt weak as if she'd injured herself and bled a great deal, and her body was trying to recuperate from the loss.

It's nearby, an alarm deep in her gut said.

Fiona stood up and rushed out the tent. She was permitted to take a break at the top of every hour so long as she put a sign on the outside of her tent, letting people know she would be back soon. She didn't put the sign up and didn't plan on being back anytime soon either. With everything going on, she was sure her boss would give her a pass. If he didn't, she wouldn't be too sad about losing this job.

Fiona was still shaking when she climbed into the driver's seat of her car, sticking the key in the ignition. She hardly wanted to glance at the windshield, afraid she would see familiar red eyes looking back at her.

Nothing.

Fiona drove home with barely any memory of doing so. In the safety of her home, she felt a little bit better, more prepared. If the demon were to sneak up on her here, she'd be ready for it. She had salt, iron, and everything else that supposedly helped to ward off an evil spirit.

Fiona did a lap around her house, gathering everything she considered valuable on the counter. A pile of her crystals sat next to her incense, a jar of salt from the kitchen, and her iron fireplace poker. For luck, she also added an anointed white candle. As she studied it over, another flash of doubt went through her. If this creature could tear itself from one world and into another, would a jar of salt really be enough to stop it?

It's gonna have to be. She shuddered at the mental image of Ally's corpse. Somehow, the flickering apparition of what was left of her ghost, her soul, was worse.

Only once she'd gathered every protective thing she owned, did she seat herself on the hard wooden kitchen chair beside her counter. She thought of the red eyes again, and all she wanted was to talk to her entity, to see what it meant for her to be able to see whatever it was in such a transparent fashion.

Fiona set both hands out. In her mind, she could picture her energy swirling out, mixing with the pile of protective trinkets to create a type of barrier that would keep her safe from anything that might interrupt her connection.

Clearing her head of everything but the entity, she started to whisper, the lights overhead flickering as if they were nothing more than the flame of a candle in the breeze. Fiona resisted opening her eyes, continuing her spell. She expected to hear that familiar *woosh*, but after she was finished, there was no sign of him. Worriedly, she chewed on her fingernails and considered what that could mean. Was the creature blocking their connection?

Could it *do* that?

Or could it be that the entity wouldn't risk coming close to her for fear the demon would notice him?

She glanced toward her refrigerator, jolting out of her seat when she realized she wasn't alone. There was a faded apparition standing there, the color so light that in most places, it simply blended into the background. She thought of Ally's spirit, the faded edges and frantic fear that she was on the verge of simply disappearing. Fiona rose to face the spirit, the way she usually did to pay her respects to those who visited her.

The apparition moved closer, coming to rest a few feet away. From the flowy gown to the almond eyes and dark hair pulled into a bun, this was the woman she'd seen in the obituary.

Madame Griselda.

Fiona didn't know what to say or do. All she could think of was the conversation she'd had with the entity when he'd assured her that she wouldn't be able to reach the woman who had given her her powers. He had lied to her.

Her guardian had *lied*.

"He said I couldn't reach you," she stuttered. "Why…how…"

"He does what he can to protect me," she said, voice surprisingly strong. "That's what his purpose is: to guard the guardians."

"I have to sit down," Fiona said, plopping onto the chair she'd risen from. She blinked once, twice, and after carefully grounding herself, looked up at the woman. "Why are you here? It's dangerous."

Unless he lied about that too.

"You doubt your abilities, and that doubt will be your downfall if you don't rein it in," she warned. "You cannot afford the distraction."

Fiona jutted out her bottom lip, caught between bitterness and stubbornness. Of course she *doubted* herself. It wasn't as if she'd had anyone to guide her powers along, to let her know everything she was capable of. To tell her the truth and tell her she wasn't crazy. Sure, her guardian had kept her *safe*, but he hadn't offered the guidance she needed.

Now, it seemed no one would.

"Well, what do you expect?" Fiona asked, flaring her nostrils indignantly. "I can't fight a *demon*. It's not as if I have *magic*.

KAYLA FREDERICK

All I can do is talk to dead people. This is a terrible gift."

"There was a time when I thought the same, but I did it, and so can you."

The lights in the house went out with a *pop*, leaving Fiona in darkness.

MEMENTO MORI

11.

FIONA REGRETTED NOT lighting the candle, but she had a feeling that it wouldn't have mattered if she had. Whatever the thing was, it was so powerful it took the energy out of *everything*.

Light included.

Fiona dove in the direction of the counter, hand slipping through the pile of supplies until she grazed the cold metal of her fireplace poker. She picked it up, holding it in both hands as she tried to detect any movement. A guttural roar made her entire living room shake, and she stumbled backward, suddenly using her weapon for balance rather than combat.

Feet firmly planted on the floor, she focused on the living room. The red eyes were back. Except now, they were larger than they'd been in the confines of her crystal ball. *Much* larger. Fiona weighed her options. Attack? Or run?

Odds are probably the same either way, she thought and charged. She would rather die fighting than die as a coward.

As soon as she stepped foot into the living room, the eyes vanished, the blackness around her swirling like a cloud of insects. Fiona spun in circles, trying to find the eyes, or anything that signified the beasts' form, but the inky mist was *everywhere*. It created a dome that pressed in closer and closer. Terrified, Fiona dropped to her knees to keep the overhead from touching her and swatted it frantically with the fire-poker. It went right through, moving sluggishly as if she'd dipped it in water.

This is it. It's going to massacre me like it did to Ally.

Blackness encroached her vision, and she wondered how

she could've failed so badly. Why had Madame Giselda believed she was strong enough to follow in her footsteps? Why did she believe Fiona could watch over the Veil, could keep her fellow neighbors safe when she couldn't even save herself?

Fiona crouched lower and lower, bending down to the point where her nose brushed the floor. There was no other place to go to escape the coming onslaught. Soft stinging ran down her back, immediately followed by a hot pain. The haze had made contact. Something rattled loose in her, an energy that buzzed through her entire body, and she let out a guttural scream as it blasted out of her.

The pain in her back diminished, healing as if the injury had never occurred.

Fiona opened her eyes, able to see enough to determine that the dome had broken. Seizing the opportunity, she jumped to her feet. Red eyes beamed at her from the shadows on the other side of the room. The demon was observing her, seizing her up for the next weakness it could exploit.

Fiona didn't feel weak anymore. With the white barrier around her, she felt a special kind of power, as if she could beat anything.

This thing included.

Fiona tossed the poker to the ground, listening to the rattle as it hit the floor. She didn't take her eyes off the demon's as she stood there, balling her hands into fists and urging the thing to attack again.

It didn't.

Fiona closed her eyes, imagining the energy around her pumping her full of strength and determination as it flowed from

MEMENTO MORI

her brain, down her throat, and into the muscles in her arms. When she opened her eyes, white balls of energy glowed on her palms.

Another guttural roar tore through her house before the demon sprang at her like a neatly coiled snake. The entity grew closer and closer, but Fiona felt no fear. Before it reached her, she lifted her hands, shoving a ball of energy into each of its eyes. The screech that it let out reminded her of nails on a chalkboard, except it was worse. Much worse. Almost like the sound of something being run over.

Fiona had a moment where she almost stopped herself. All it took was the memory of Ally's body splayed out on the dirt floor of her tent for Fiona to refocus. The creature transformed from haze to an almost humanoid shape with long claws and bat-like wings.

It didn't keep the form long before it changed again to a thing with two rows of teeth. Fiona gritted her teeth, trying to keep up the barrage, but she was starting to tire, and guessed the creature was doing its best to harness energy from her each time they made contact. Her insides ached, pain starting in her heart and moving throughout her muscles to the very tips of her fingers.

She wouldn't be able to hold on much longer.

Seconds counted down in her mind, but the creature continued its attacks. It roared and tried to get past her extended hands. In a last-ditch effort to save herself, she forced every ounce of white haze out of her, launching it through the air and into the creature's chest. When the wisp disappeared, her world tilted, and she collapsed to her knees, staring at the spot where it vanished.

In her ear, her guardian said, "You did it."

KAYLA FREDERICK

MEMENTO MORI

Smile to hide the darkness of your thoughts.

KAYLA FREDERICK

MEMENTO MORI

The Day You Killed Me

1.

ON THE FIRST night of fall, Brian and Rosa Murphy settled in for the evening like every other couple on the block. Brian was already in bed, remote control in hand, as he flicked aimlessly through channels while his wife pulled her drab nightgown over her head. Brian kept his eyes on the television, thumb pressing the button like a zombie. Rosa paced from the closet to the bathroom, staring at her reflection in the mirror as she poked at all her blemishes and imperfections.

Brian landed on a local station broadcasting a beauty pageant. Brian's own daughter, Caroline, filled the screen, beaming as the gold crown was placed on her head. Rosa halted in the bathroom door, proudly watching Caroline take her practiced steps up to the microphone, ready to give her all during her acceptance speech.

"Beautiful, as always," she said approvingly.

Brian nodded in agreement.

"But her walk is a little sloppy," Rosa added, face contorting in disgust as she slid into bed beside him.

"Maybe it's the shoes."

"It's not the shoes," Rosa said bitterly. Those shoes had been *her* decision, and she wasn't wrong. Not when it came to the pageant world. "She wants to drag her feet, and I've told her and told her not to do that. It's no good for her posture. Her lessons will be first tomorrow."

Brian agreed and stretched his thumb across the remote to hit the power button, successfully blackening the screen before Rosa could voice any more complaints. In another world, maybe things were more relaxed. In this one? They had a reputation to keep. Their daughters Caroline, Daytona, and Victoria were all pageant stars carrying their own win streaks, and the only way to ensure they would stay on track were harsh punishments, long training sessions, and a strict diet.

The phone rang, disrupting Brian as he drifted off to sleep. "Who could be calling at this hour?" he grumbled with Rosa's piercing glare scorching the side of his face. She said nothing as he picked up the receiver. "Hello?" he bellowed, hoping whoever was on the receiving end would feel his displeasure.

"I'm coming home, Daddy," a girl said. Open air whooshed through the phone, and before he could think of a response, the line clicked and went dead.

The bitterness around Rosa's eyes dissolved into some shade of worry as she said. "What is it?"

"She's alive."

Rosa went as pale as her husband. Could it be that the daughter they had buried, hadn't actually been dead?

MEMENTO MORI

2.

IT'S NOT THE darkness or the calm that stirs me from the place of nothingness, but rather the material pressed against my face like a second layer of skin. It covers my eyes, and when I open my mouth, it clings to my lips, threatening to go down my throat with each breath. I turn my head, and it caresses my nostrils. Plastic. A thin layer of it. No matter how I move, it's there, encasing me, hiding me. I gasp again, panic starting to bubble in my throat when I can't clear the sensation.

Opening my eyes only makes it worse because I can't see. My breathing intensifies, and I have the feeling if I don't quell it, it will knock me out. I'm sure if that happens, I won't wake again. I slap the plastic from my face. It barely moves before snapping back against my skin, cradling me. I look up, hoping to see an escape from this prison, but there is none. It's the same darkness from every angle. My fingers fly through the air above my head only to be halted by the plastic again.

I'm *in* it.

A trashbag, I know this with a certainty I didn't have a moment prior.

Then the panic comes back, as I imagine my oxygen supply dwindling. I claw through the plastic, the bag giving with a quiet *rippp*. Fresh air greets me, and I take short rapid breaths until my heart rate stabilizes. I look up at the sky, trying to gain a sense of location. Black branches sprout through the purple sky, but they're not enough to block out the moon and the stars. I watch them as I compose myself because it's much easier to look at something familiar than this...whatever *this* is.

Dropping my gaze, I study my immediate surroundings but none of it is familiar. Not that *any* woods would be to me. It's nearly impossible to see through the undergrowth at this time of night, but I have the feeling that if I could see, it wouldn't make much difference.

I knit my eyebrows and twist my toes, the slight movement stirring the plastic that sits in tatters around me. In the slight breeze, it crinkles but doesn't drift away. I run a strip through my fingers with a sudden realization—someone had *thrown me away.*

But who and why?

More importantly, how am I still alive?

MEMENTO MORI

3.

"HOW COULD THIS have happened?" Rosa demanded, glaring at Brian with everything she had in her. When she was angry, she was no longer the beautiful woman he'd married. She was a hellcat, a demon, and he was positive she'd taken his soul at some point in their life together. "You promised it was taken care of."

Brian wasn't sure what to say. He continued to stare at the dead phone in his hand as if it would suddenly come to life and answer the question if he wished hard enough.

"What if she goes to the police?" Rosa continued, hands on her hips and expression on her face that made her appear fifteen years older, at least. "That will be the end of us."

Brian's face contorted with a mix of anger and grief. He didn't want to think about himself, not with the memory of the terrible thing he had done. It didn't seem important, and the fact that Rosa could approach the situation with any sort of selfishness made his stomach twist.

"She was dead," Brian said firmly. He remembered the feeling of Blythe's windpipe beneath his fingers, remembered the *pop* it had made when he pressed, the way the cords and tendons had stretched and struggled to protect her ability to breathe then had all gone still the moment of her last breath.

"Apparently, she *wasn't*," Rosa said, shaking her head as if she were more disgusted by him than the heinous crime. "I knew I should've gotten someone more experienced."

"Someone more experienced? Really? Because you have so many people like that at your beck and call?" Brian snapped, unable to take the barrage anymore.

Rosa's eyes narrowed, her face taking on the look of a hawk before it scoops up an unsuspecting mouse. "Not…at the moment. But they exist. I don't need to tell you twice."

"She was dead," Brian repeated because all the anger in the world wouldn't take back what he had done. He could still remember the light leaving Blythe's eyes, how her body had stilled. The moment he had gone from having four daughters to three.

"Well, get dressed," she said, throwing on a heavy robe and grabbing her tennis shoes.

"Why?"

"We have to find her," Rosa said, exasperated. "And make sure she stays buried this time."

Brian watched her, hardly able to believe this woman was the same woman who had once adored her family, the one who never wanted to hurt a fly.

Knocking sounded at the door, quiet at first, but louder and more persistent as it stretched on. Rosa's narrowed eyes went wide. Brian rose from the bed, glancing toward the doorway as if he expected his dead daughter to suddenly appear there.

"Looks like *she's* found *us*."

MEMENTO MORI

4.

IT'S HARD TO decide what the worst part of this is—the ten minutes I sit in absolute silence or when I remember everything that happened and can do nothing to change it. My father's eyes, that's all I can see. The lack of remorse, the absolute *coldness*. I shake my head, twin tears running down my cheeks, but the more I try to deny it, the harder it hits.

I'm supposed to be dead. Running the plastic strips through my fingers is reminder enough, a reminder that my own father had tried to throw me away.

I'm in my grave.

I swallow, and it hurts. The points of my throat where my father's fingers had pressed are alive with throbbing aches, and I'm confused again. Dead people don't hurt, right? Death is supposed to be peaceful, simple. I've heard of out of body experiences, people looking down on their bodies from some impossible distance, but this doesn't seem like that. Things are *tangible*. I don't want to touch the trash bag, but it reminds me that I'm real.

I look at my hands, my body, my legs. My pale skin glows in the darkness, and I stare at it as I take in more fresh air, expanding my lungs as far as they will go.

Air is precious.

What I'd once thought of as an infinite resource is now worth more to me than gold. My throat feels dry, and I lift my hand warily before waving it in my face. What is this existence? Am I alive? Am I dead? Am I somewhere in between?

I don't know, and I don't know how to go about finding the answer. I pinch my arm. The skin gives and snaps back into place. It turns red, but there's no pain. I try to tell myself it's because all the pain is in my throat, and in my mind, but that doesn't quite satisfy my questions.

What does that mean? I ask myself, but know I can't dwell on that question either.

I had lived a lifetime full of pain, so some small part of me revels in the thought that I can exist without it for a little while, even if I don't quite understand why it's happening.

MEMENTO MORI

5.

BRIAN AND ROSA held their breath, the unspoken agreement that they would wait out whoever was out there in the air, but the knocking showed no signs of stopping. Opening the door, facing what would be on the other side, terrified Brian more than he would let himself admit.

"Should we open the door?" Brian asked at last.

Rosa *hmphed*, nose in the air as she stormed past him. He didn't try to interfere, instead following her out into the hallway. As the man of the house, he should've led the charge, but he was afraid. So instead, he'd let Rosa take the reins, let her see the daughter she had insisted was better off dead.

She marched through the living room as the banging on the door grew louder and louder. Rosa grabbed the knob, but before she pulled the door open, the sound stopped. She froze in the sudden silence. When Brian made no suggestions, she peered through the peephole, unmoving as she scanned the porch and the yard beyond the door.

Waiting for her to speak was the longest minute of Brian's life. "Well? What do you see?" he demanded when the silence became unbearable.

"Nothing," she replied. "There's no one here."

"That's impossib—" The crash of glass from the kitchen interrupted the rest of his sentence.

KAYLA FREDERICK

6.

I WALK THROUGH the trees for what feels like hours, but I have no way to tell how long it's actually been. I have no sense of time—what is time when you're dead anyway? I'm cold, and I attempt to warm up by hugging myself. When I think too much of the gesture, however, I drop it. There's nothing sadder than being that lonely.

Except loneliness is not new to me. I grew up in a relatively large family—three sisters, a mother, and a father—but I've never felt close to any of them. Probably the one who understood me the most was ironically my father. Tears well in my eyes, and as I wander through the forest, resisting the urge to hug myself again, I feel a whole new level of embarrassment.

How did my life come to this?

Be strong. I breathe deep, but the sting in my eyes warns me my body has no interest in obeying.

On a loop, I picture my father's eyes as he squeezed the life out of me. It's hard to believe that the person who helped give me life, the one who kissed my booboos, and listened to me cry, could be a stranger. Fifteen years I had been part of his and Momma's life, and that had all been wiped away in the unpleasantness of one evening.

Monsters really do look like everyday people.

I think of my sisters and wonder what's become of them. It wasn't usual for all of us to be home at the same time, but that night was different. My sisters had been snoozing away in their bedrooms upstairs as I slipped away to blackness in the dusty old

MEMENTO MORI

basement.

    I purse my lips, worried that if I bite them, I'll chew right through. What do my sisters know of my death? Do they know what happened? Or do they assume I'm missing? What have my parents told people? I'm sure there's been questions. We had been too well known in our little strip of urban paradise for there to be none, even about *me*, the black sheep of the family.

KAYLA FREDERICK

7.

EVERY OUNCE OF bravery Brian and Rosa might have had vanished. They stared at each other, neither one wanting to make the first move. Whoever had been at the door was inside now, and soon, that meant they'd be face-to-face with them, regardless of what they did.

Despite the violent crime Brian had committed, and Rosa had conspired, they weren't used to atrocities being committed *to* them. They were the couple everyone loved, admired, cherished. They'd never had so much as a disagreement with their neighbors.

What felt like an eternity later, Brian broke from the trance and hurried to fling open the basement door. A baseball bat lurked in the corner. His fingers wrapped around it, and Rosa screamed. Brian rushed to the living room, desperate to be at her side, to save her and put an end to this situation once and for all.

When he got to the living room, however, Brian did none of those things. He froze up, like a deer in the headlights, and stared at his daughter with the butcher knife in her hand.

MEMENTO MORI

8.

I'D ALWAYS BEEN a big believer in Karma. That people who have been bad, people who have wronged others, people who have evil in their hearts will eventually receive the bad energy they put out into the world.

So how did this fate fall to me?

I'm not a bad person. Or at least, I don't think I am. I've done things I'm not proud of, but who hasn't? I always knew I was the black sheep of the family. My sisters, for better or worse, are basically all copies of the same person. They follow orders and go along with whatever our parents decide. They are happy with the way their life is.

I'd been the only one who hated the pageant life—the makeup, the Vaseline smiles, and the elegant hairstyles filled with so many pins and clips that we were guaranteed a grandiose migraine by the end of the night.

From little children on, my sisters and I had been dressed up, showed off. My entire life was a never-ending pageant. I would be reminded of my etiquette at the dinner table and my posture when I walked. My living Hell had been my Mom's favorite hobby.

It bothered me more that I was the only one to see through it. The only one who wanted something different. My sisters enjoyed the spotlight, the attention. It made them feel special. Validated.

I was never made for that life.

I am the first one in my family to ever lose a pageant, and

the only one to have a losing *streak*. After every pageant I lost, I was beaten by my mother, marks left in places that wouldn't be detectable in photos. The first time it happened, I was little…so little that I hated myself more than her. But once the beatings became a regular occurrence, I started to care less. Maybe that was what had really sealed my fate, or maybe it had been something else entirely. Some other taboo I hadn't known existed.

Mom wanted dolls she could groom and perfect, beautiful beings who would smile and not talk back, but I'm not the porcelain variety that my sisters appear to be.

No.

I'm more like Annabelle.

MEMENTO MORI

9.

"HONEY, *HONEY!*" ROSA soothed, a terrified chuckle passing her lips.

The girl inched closer, lip pulled back into a snarl.

"Put the knife down, honey, so we can talk about this," Rosa tried again but did not succeed. The knife stayed extended above the girl's head as if she was deciding which parent she wanted to kill more.

"Why should I do that?" she said. "Why should I listen to anything you tell me? They're lies, aren't they? They're *all* lies."

"That's not true," Brian tried to say, but his voice quavered.

A feral sound tore up the girl's throat, and she angled toward Brian as if she'd decided she would start with him.

"It's alright. We can talk about this," Brian mimicked his wife, extending his arms in an effort at a peaceful gesture, but she wasn't hearing it.

Her eyes lingered on the baseball bat tucked in the crook of his arm. "If that's the truth, you'll put down the bat."

Brian hesitated, unsure how to proceed. There was something off in the glint of his daughter's eyes, something familiar. Monsters recognized one another. He moved to drop the bat, the smooth surface passing through his hands before he paused. There was a voice warning him not to do it, that giving in was dangerous, but Rosa's eyes were wide as she looked between her husband and their daughter so fast that her face was a blur of movement. Brian could read her expression—she wanted him to listen to their girl. She was—perhaps—eviler than him, but she was also innocent in a way. In thinking the situation could resolve amicably, she had handed over any hope of making it through the night.

"Sweetheart, it's late. How about we get some rest and talk about this in the morning?" Rosa suggested, tone hopeful.

"No. There's not going to be a morning for any of us."

Rosa let out a bewildered chuckle. "Th-that's silly, honey."

"Is it?" she asked, eyeing the bat in Brian's arm again. "I know what you did. I know what happened."

Rosa blanched. "What do you mean?"

"Drop the damn bat is what I mean!" the girl hissed.

Rosa shot Brian a scornful look but added no words. With a sigh, Brian let go, and the bat clattered to the ground.

Their daughter watched, pleased, and gave a wide pageant smile to show off all her perfect teeth. It said to *relax* though they knew they weren't safe to do so.

MEMENTO MORI

10.

THE LONGER I walk, the more memories of my last few hours of life come back to me. The pain reignites my fire, my strength to fight, my will to live, but at the same time, it hurts so goddamn bad that I don't know how I'll ever cope with it.

The Harvest Pageant was a nightmare time in my life. I was used to vigorous training for local pageants, but for county ones? State ones? No. And Rosa wasn't either, it seemed. She second-guessed herself constantly, going so far as to make me change multiple times over until she was satisfied. I don't want to talk about how much preparation went into my hair and nails.

By the time we arrived at the pageant, my mind was shot. I smiled only after Rosa rubbed my teeth with Vaseline. Somehow, despite my sarcastic responses to everything, I won. Cheers rose around me, but it was as if I was caught in a glass box, separated from the full effect. I could see Rosa in the crowd, loudly declaring that *"I was her baby."* And something in me snapped. Everything about this was wrong. Fake. Outside of these moments, Rosa was *never* proud of me. In my entire life, I couldn't remember a time when she'd told me she loved me.

The host set the crown on my head, and I accepted the microphone, using it to loudly tell him go fuck himself before I threw the crown to the ground.

Deathly silence filled the building as I shouted into the microphone, "The grass on the other side looks greener because it's fake!"

Mom and Dad had been so angry the entire way home, I

KAYLA FREDERICK

wasn't sure what to do. They say to always listen to your gut, and in the silence of that car ride, mine told me that something was wrong, but I pushed it away. No one in their right mind thinks their parents will kill them, but I've learned the hard way to always expect the unexpected.

Up ahead, I see a break in the trees and run for it, glad to be out of what could've been my final resting place. In the city, the streetlights are bright enough to hurt my eyes. It's late, and there's no one around. I have a hard time deciding if that's a good thing or not. Cutting across the lawn of the library, I spot the newspaper boxes out front and pause at a picture of me.

I rush to it. *They don't put your picture in the paper for being gone one day*, I think, and puff with a swell of sickness as I scan the story, searching for some clue of how long I've been in the forest.

I start to read:

Authorities are still on the lookout for missing fifteen-year-old Blythe Owens who disappeared the night of the seventeenth, hours after returning home from the Harvest Pageant with her parents. No word has risen as to her whereabouts and police have asked if anyone has information to please come forward.

The Owens are well-known for their history of pageant dominance in Water County. While there is no evidence suggesting anything more than a runaway situation, all pageants have been delayed until all possible leads have been exhausted.

Mother Rosa Owens says, "If anyone has seen my beautiful daughter, please come forward. Our family is not complete without her."

MEMENTO MORI

They killed me and used it for attention, I think with a disgusted groan. I'm a bomb of emotion ready to explode, a kaleidoscope of impossible to decipher feelings.

What would happen if someone saw me now, if I were rounded up by the police and brought back to my parents? Lips pressed into a straight line, I hurry to the phone booth across the street. When the doors close behind me, I feel as if I'm in the trash bag again, and it makes me want to scream.

With shaking fingers, I pick up the receiver, listening to the dial tone before I finally convince myself to punch in the number. This is the closest thing to a plan I can imagine right now.

I tell myself, *"They have no right to do this."* Then *"I deserve better,"* and *"They need to pay."*

It doesn't make this task any easier.

"Hello," the voice says on the other end of the line.

I freeze, thinking back to those last moments before my death. Squeezing my eyes shut, I force it away and say, "I'm coming home, Daddy."

11.

TO WIN A beauty pageant, it's not enough to be beautiful—you have to be smart, articulate, and talented. A Goddess, come to walk the Earth.

Those were all traits the daughter was glad she had as she dashed across the room, movements graceful like she was dancing, a moment before she shoved the knife through Rosa's neck. All the fitness training she'd been through had given her strength that neither parent could've anticipated. Rosa's eyes streamed water as she tried to reach up, to pull out the knife, but she had no chance as her own blood poured down the front of her shirt and into her lungs, drowning her. She made a series of clicking gasps that caused the daughter to grin, dipping her foot in the crimson puddle to smear it across the floor.

"What have you done?" Brian asked.

"I'm painting, Daddy. Just look how talented I am!" she exclaimed and continued to make a collage of bloody footprints.

Brian tried to duck around the dancing girl, to get to his wife's side as the blood doubled beneath her body, but the daughter darted into his path every time. Seeing no other option, Brian scooped up the bat, charging toward his attacker.

Easily, she ducked and twisted, planting the knife in the middle of her father's back as she completed her effortless ballerina twirl. The old man crumpled to the floor, gasping and choking for air beside the bloody corpse of his wife, the baseball bat landing beside him with a thump. The daughter watched on, entranced by his struggles, and wondered how long he would live

MEMENTO MORI

if she left the knife in his spine.

"I told you to drop the bat, Daddy," she said.

KAYLA FREDERICK

12.

BY THE TIME my old home comes into view, I've shed the weakest parts of myself. All that anguish and pain? It's like they never existed. Everything else is locked away behind anger. I'm here on a mission, and no matter what, I won't leave until that mission is complete.

Clenching my hands into fists, I step onto the porch and raise my hand as if I'm about to knock when I freeze. A resounding echo plays in the back of my mind—I died here. It's hard to breathe, and for the smallest hint of a second, I fear I'm back in the bag in the woods. My vision blurs, and I try not to cry. After a moment, the hallucination passes, and I stare at my raised fist then the door.

Should I knock? Or barge in?

Barge in of course.

The door is unlocked and swings on its hinges with a tiny creak I've become all too accustomed to. The light in the living room is on, but there's no one there. I stand in the doorway, unsure how to proceed. Do I announce myself or pretend everything is normal and see how long it takes my parents to realize I'm not dead?

I open my mouth, ready to say something when a red puddle staining the carpet catches my attention. Shaking, I crouch down beside it. The iron tang of blood reaches my nose, and I hop to my feet, mind racing with horrible images I wish I could forget.

What if Rosa and Brian turned their wrath on my sisters?

MEMENTO MORI

What if I wasn't the only one they decided they were done with?

There's a trail of crimson dots leading away from this puddle, and against my better judgment, I follow it. The stains get bigger and bigger as I go up the stairs and down the hall toward my parents' room. I don't want to take another step, but I can't stop myself. Gathering my last scrap of courage, I peek inside, not prepared for the sight that greets me.

KAYLA FREDERICK

13.

DAYTONA, MY ONLY older sister, is singing, "You are my Sunshine." On an ordinary day, that wouldn't be unusual. Out of all of us, she has the most beautiful voice, and she's always blurting out cheesy songs. But this isn't an ordinary day, nor is the way she's singing; an odd and off-key rendition that makes it almost…*ominous.*

I watch from the doorway, so silent she takes no notice. Her back is to me from where she sits on the edge of the bed, her long blonde hair falling to the blankets beneath her. Crimson dots the space beside her, and I remember my frantic dash up here. The blood leads to Daytona, but she doesn't seem harmed.

There's a makeup brush in her hand, and her singing gets louder as she dips it in the container of blush in her other hand. She taps it gently, removing the excess makeup then holds it up to the thing beside her.

Mom and Dad are lying there, their blood seeping through the blankets and their eyes wide in the endless stare of death. Their faces are caked in a heavy layer of makeup, the blush the last touch on mom's cheek before Daytona sets the brush down and claps her hands together.

"Now, aren't you just *beautiful?* Tell me, what's your talent?" she asks, holding a hairbrush to Mom's lifeless face as if it's a microphone. "Oh, oh! How wonderful!" Daytona cheers and tilts her head to the side, the tips of her blonde hair sliding through the blood to darken them. "And how do you feel about world hunger?"

MEMENTO MORI

I can't hold my tongue anymore. "Daytona," I say with little to no emotion, mostly because I don't know what tone will work for this scene. Shock? Empathy? Fear? *Gratitude?* I'd felt a lot toward my parents, but this? I don't think even I could've been capable of this.

Daytona gasps and turns toward me, eyes wide, exaggerated by the heavy mascara and fake eyelashes she's wearing. Tears bubble up, smearing makeup above and below each eye. "Blythe! I never thought I'd see you again!" she says, standing up off the bed.

The compact falls to the ground, pink dust staining the carpet around it in a powdery puddle.

"What did you do, Daytona?" I ask, taking the smallest step toward her.

Her lips quiver and her chin drops as she lifts her arms, waiting for me to return the hug. The look in her eyes tells me she knows the truth—what Mom and Dad had done. We embrace, murderess and murdered. She's tiny, so much tinier than I remember, and that's no doubt thanks to Mom's "one meal a day policy."

"You're alive," she says in my ear.

"I'm alive," I repeat.

She pulls away and leaves a smear of blood on my arm. I look at it then her and say, "I know the perfect dumping spot."

KAYLA FREDERICK

MEMENTO MORI

We're no different, you and I. I just wear my demons on the outside.

KAYLA FREDERICK

MEMENTO MORI

Secrets of the Quiet Visitor

1.

I'VE ALWAYS BEEN a light sleeper, which can be both a blessing and a curse. Staying asleep is difficult, but sometimes that comes in handy. Like when someone smashes in my kitchen window. Heart thudding, I hop out of bed, giving the empty mattress a scathing glance. My husband should be here with me, but he's not. He's out on a business trip…or so he says, anyway. Whatever waits for me in the kitchen, I'll have to handle on my own.

Ducking into the shadows of the closet, I listen for movement from elsewhere in the house. *Creak.* The intruder is moving down the hall. I pull the dusty box from the back of the shelf. There's a revolver inside, and I pluck it out, loading it with six bullets before I snap the chamber back into place.

The gun feels heavy and awkward in my hands. The last time I'd handled it was the day I bought it. My thumb fumbles to get the safety off, and as I go into the hall, I nearly bump right into the intruder. He's dressed in all black, with a ski mask over his face, but I can tell he's a man by the size of his frame, his build so much like that of my absent husband.

"Freeze!" I shout.

He doesn't listen, of course, and tries to lunge at me. On instinct, my finger slips to the trigger, and I pull it. One loud gunshot rings out. He falls to his knees, but I don't move. I stare down at the man lying across my hallway carpet, a pool of blood circling him.

"Who are you?" I demand, keeping the gun trained on him as if he could possibly get back up.

He doesn't answer, a groan making its way out of his chest, low and subtle. "Please, I'm sorry."

"Answer my question."

"My name is Morgan, please. I'm hurt bad," he says.

"I know," I reply, pulling the hammer back with a click. "And you're about to hurt more if you don't tell me why you're in my home."

"I'm desperate. I saw your house and I…I…" he trails off. Before I can ask another question, he rips the ski-mask off, staring up at me through bloodshot eyes. A trickle of blood runs from the corner of his mouth, and he's pale, so pale I wonder if he's about to faint.

"And you thought *what*? That you could come in here and take me for the little I have?"

He groans again, and the sound makes me *angry*. It's almost as if he expects me to take pity on him after what he'd been about to do.

Well, that's *not* going to happen.

"Please…I need you to-to call 911," he says, lifting his hand to show the dark blood smeared on his palm and fingers.

I drop down by his side, gun pointed directly between his eyes. "Now why would I do that? No one else knows you're here."

"Ple—" he starts to beg again.

I don't want to hear it, hear *him*. Before he finishes

MEMENTO MORI

speaking, I crack the barrel of the gun against his temple.

He goes unconscious.

I stare at his body. This is not how I planned my night going. I need my sleep—my day had been long enough—but this isn't a situation I can ignore. Now, *I'm* the one groaning as I tuck the gun into the waistband of my pajama bottoms and stick my hands under his armpits. He's too heavy to lift so I drag him, a thin trail of blood following us, staining the carpet the entire way. When we make it to the end of the hall, I drop him with a *thump* and pull open the door.

It's dark, the faint light from the window at the end of the hall illuminating the top two stairs before the rest are plunged in darkness. I smack the switch with my hand, and the basement light comes on. I pick up my guest under the armpits once again, grunting under the weight, and drag him to the top of the stairs before I let him go, watching his body roll downward with morbid curiosity. Only once he comes to rest at the bottom do I begin my descent. I step around him to go into the basement, approaching the chair sitting in the middle of the room. Before I reach it, I step over a bundle.

As an afterthought I tack on, "Hi, Katherine."

She doesn't respond. Not that I expected her to. The blanket around her face is crusted with dried blood. I've forgotten how long she's been down here. Two days? Three?

I pick up the chair and step back over her before I head to Morgan, still lying crumpled at the base of the stairs. It seems as if there's more blood leaking out of him now. The willpower some people have to survive always surprises me.

"You're a fighter," I tell him, almost admiringly.

KAYLA FREDERICK

With massive effort, I heave his body up onto the chair. He falls to the side, and I catch him. Using the handrail beside the stairs, I prop him up before I move to my shelves, searching for ropes. I tie him to the chair and step back to admire my work. In the eerie light, I'm drawn again to his complexion, so much like porcelain. He's almost perfect, except I don't like how close to the stairs the chair is. Licking my teeth, I grab the wooden back and pull it across the room, the legs *scraping* against the floor the entire way.

By the time the chair is positioned in the center of the room, I'm exhausted. I sit on the bottom step, resting my elbows on my knees. Blood covers my hands and pajamas. This is nothing short of inconvenient, and I almost have a moment where I feel bad for this, for *him,* but then my gaze goes to Katherine.

There's no regret there. She's the reason my husband isn't here right now. He says it's a business trip, but I know *she's* been the one on the other end.

Then my eyes move to the bleeding man in the chair. Now that he's here, I'm not sure what to do with him. I could leave him alone, and he'll bleed out, but there doesn't seem to be a great deal of sport in that. I've only planned to do two murders in my life—number one, Katherine, has already been done, but number two was supposed to be my husband. In my head, my plan had seemed so straightforward, and it would've been without Morgan's interference.

I'm angry again. What is it with men thinking they can take advantage of me? That they can use me for all they can before leaving me in ruins? I stand up so fast I nearly get a headrush before I move over to the man. Rearing my arm back, I slap him across the face with as much fury as I can muster. His head snaps to the side from the impact, but he doesn't stir. A blossom of red erupts on his pale cheek, but it's not enough. I want to see *more* red. I glance at the blood-crusted tools on the table by the wall.

They were the way that Katherine met her end. It had come too quickly, only a few slashes, a river of blood, and the light inside her was gone forever. Looking at Morgan tells me he'll be a bit more durable. The bullet inside him can attest to that. The more I stare at him, the more I'm reminded again about the similarity in size to my husband. That speaks to some part of me, and suddenly, I'm *glad* this man broke his way into my life.

He can be my practice doll.

Smiling, I reach out to grasp him under the chin, bringing his face up. "Wake up."

He doesn't stir.

"Wake up!" I howl, pinching his face harder.

I shake his head from side to side, and at last, a groan travels up his throat. His eyes flutter open.

"Good morning," I tell him, and let go.

"Wh-what's going on? A...are the police coming?" he mumbles.

"No, we don't need to involve them," I tell him and step to the side.

It's not a big move, but it's enough for him to see the body lying on the floor. His eyes go wide, and he tries to pull himself off the chair, but the ropes hold him tight. His face turns red with his desperate attempts to escape before he slumps in his seat.

"No. Please," he says, wide brown eyes watching my every move. "Why are you doing this?"

I shrug and walk toward the table with my knives.

"What do you want?" he screams after me.

I pick up my favorite knife, a paring blade with a purple handle, and approach him, knife extended point first. "I *wanted* to get a good night's sleep, but you were the death of that," I say with an agitated twitch of my nose.

"Please, if you let me go, I won't tell anyone what I've seen. I promise."

I suck in a breath through my teeth. "See, here's the thing. I *could* let you go, but you came into my house, so it's ultimately my decision to do with you as I see fit. And *I* want to practice on you."

"P-practice?" he stammers, wiggling against his binds subtly, as if he thinks that will somehow free him.

I touch my finger to the edge of the blade. It's sharp. So sharp that it effortlessly draws a drop of my blood. "You see our friend over there in the blanket?" I ask, gesturing to Katherine. "She tried to take something from me too—my husband."

I'm next to him by the time my sentence ends, and I slash, punctuating my words by cutting a line across his cheek. He yelps and tries to pull away. This time, I let him, holding up the blade to study the streak of crimson against the silver.

"She wasn't much of a plaything," I tell him. "Bled out far too quickly. I don't want to make the same mistakes with my husband. I want him to...*understand* the pain he caused me. Lucky for me, you happened to show up."

"I'm sorry for what your husband did, I am, but I'm not him. This isn't fair!"

"*Life's* not fair," I tell him and scoop up the rag beside my tools.

    I stuff it into his mouth until his eyes begin to water. When the knife cuts into his flesh again, he screams until he goes red in the face.

KAYLA FREDERICK

2.

HOURS LATER, I'M left staring at the dead body tied to the chair. There's a puddle of blood on the floor beneath it, and I kick myself for not putting down plastic or something to soak it up. No matter. I have a sizable bottle of bleach under my kitchen sink that should come in handy for this exact problem.

As I stare at this shell of a man, I run through a list of things that this experience has taught me. The first is that grown men *can* and *will* scream like a little girl if a situation calls for it. Hell, sometimes they do that when it *doesn't*. Second, I've learned that it takes quite a while for blood loss to take over if I space out the timings of my slashes. Last but not least, I've learned that more shallow cuts equal more pain in the end since he stayed conscious longer to feel them.

It wasn't a satisfying death. Hardly dignified. One minute he was a pain in my ass, and the next he was quiet. It almost looked as if he had drifted off to sleep, and that's not what I want for my husband.

I cut the ropes, and Morgan's body hits the cement floor with a *thump*. I wrap him in a blanket, letting his body come to a rest by Katherine's. Now I have *two* human burritos to worry about. I glance at the blood and the chair. I consider cleaning it all up, but it seems like a waste of effort when I'll spill more blood here soon anyway.

"Goodnight," I murmur to the bodies as I step over them and ascend the stairs to catch up on much-needed sleep.

MEMENTO MORI

3.

I WAKE UP refreshed and ready for what the day will bring. In the basement, Morgan's blood has coagulated to a brown circle of sludge. I hardly pay it attention as I take inventory of my tools and weapons. I'm still not satisfied with the way he died, and I know that means more experimentation once I get hubby in the chair.

In the meantime, I go to work *Dextering* the place. When I'm finished, the room is nearly shining with plastic wrap. Confident that everything is in position, I cross the room to Katherine's body. Her ugly purse is nearby, her cellphone inside. I've used it several times over the past few days to offset any suspicion, and I'll dispose of it properly when I'm done, but for now, I need it again.

I scroll through to Matthew's number. *Please come home,* I text him.

The phone lights up with a call, and I curl my lip at the picture of Matthew on the screen. His brown hair, green eyes, easy smile. A beautiful person on the outside but looking into those eyes tells another story. The call stops, and the picture of him vanishes with it. Dots appear then, *Katherine, I'm worried. Answer me.*

I shut the phone off and go up the stairs, waiting patiently by the door for Matthew's homecoming.

KAYLA FREDERICK

4.

I'M NEARLY BOUNCING with excitement when I hear the car pull into the driveway. My brain is a chaotic explosion of possibilities. I pull my gun out of the waistband of my pants and hold it up.

Too dramatic, I tell myself and tuck it back into hiding as the door pops open.

"Welcome home, honey," I say, throwing my arms open for a hug.

Matthew's eyes are wide, and he takes a step backward, fingers clenching into the white door frame. "Andrea, what are you doing here?"

I giggle and bat my eyelashes. "Waiting for you to come home, silly."

Matthew swallows, his Adam's apple bobbing with exaggerated effort as his eyes volley around the room. "Where's Katherine?" he asks quietly.

"We don't have to worry about her anymore," I say, studying every detail of his expression, a shift between fear and uncertainty, a delicate pull of his eyebrows and a slight quiver of his upper lip.

"Andrea, what have you done? Where's my wife? Where's Katherine?"

He's already rushing down the hall as the questions fly out of him. When he sees Morgan's blood on the carpet, he moves quicker, and I recognize what's fueling him—desperation. Each door he passes, he pushes open with determination as if he thinks there's a chance he can still save her.

Poor fool.

"Katherine!" he howls.

I pull the gun out. It doesn't seem too dramatic now. His expression shifts from sorry, to fear, to something altogether unreadable.

"Andrea, please, you're not well."

"*I'm* not well?" I scoff, swinging the gun around wildly. "*You're* not well! You don't recognize your own wife!"

"Andrea," he pleads, holding his hands out. "Please, give me the gun, and we can talk about this."

I aim the gun for his abdomen in the same way I had Morgan. If he could survive the bullet, Matthew will too. "There's nothing to talk about."

"Please, just give me the gun," he says again and takes the tiniest step forward.

I hold the weapon tighter, nostrils flaring.

"Okay, okay, you can keep it, but I need you to talk to me. Tell me what's happened." He takes another step forward, and I cock the hammer back.

I would be foolish to think this situation could be resolved peacefully, so I aim to be the first to turn this to violence. I will *not* let him get the upper hand.

Not again.

"What's the last thing you remember?" Matthew asks softly.

I scrunch my face. "The last thing I *remember* is finding that awful bitch in our bed. *Our* bed."

His eyes go wide again. "Andrea, please. You don't live

here…you've never lived here."

"You lie!" I shriek, and to my horror, tears bubble in the corners of my eyes.

"Please, tell me where Katherine is," he whispers.

The tears harden. How can this man not see how much he's hurt me? How can he not care? *Well, I am capable of the same cruelty.* "You want to see your whore? Fine."

I pull the trigger, and he collapses to the floor, blood leaking onto the carpet not far from the puddle that Morgan had left. Since I don't trust Matthew to not make a grab for my gun, I keep it in one hand, using the other to grab him by the top of the arm. Pulling him down the hallway like that takes more effort, but I know it hurts him as much as it hurts me. I can feel the tissues and muscles threatening to pop out of place as his body pulls against itself. If I happened to dislocate his shoulder, that would be icing on the cake.

When we reach the basement door, I push it open. "You want to see her? Go see!" I howl and kick him down the stairs.

His body rolling down to a rest sounds like a carpet more than a living being. Morgan's descent had been more graceful. Or maybe I'm biased. I creep down a minute later, expecting him to have passed out from the shock, but he's conscious. His eyes are all for Katherine. Tears roll down his cheeks, and I wonder which hurts more—physical pain or emotional.

"No, no, no," he moans over and over as if that'll change anything.

He's so wrapped in his grief that he doesn't struggle as I grab him by the top of the arm again and drag him toward the chair. As his body slides across the floor, I take note of the awkward angle of his left leg. It looks broken. "This is a disgusting display, you know."

"How could you do this to her?" he asks.

"It wasn't as if it was difficult. She always did love her sleeping pills. How could she ever hear someone approach when she was unconscious?"

I drop him to the plastic, his blood smearing across the clear surface. He continues to cry, and I want to slap him, to get the tears to stop. He hasn't lived with dignity, the least he could do is *try* to die with it, but I guess that's out the window.

"Who's the other one?" he asks, sniffling.

I stare down at him coldly, debating the answer. I could lie and make that emotional pain inside him so much worse, but I suddenly have no desire to do so. Not when my prey seems ready to kill itself already. I consider walking away and leaving him down here with his broken leg and the dead body of his beloved. It'd be interesting to see if someone can really die of a broken heart, but then I wouldn't get to see much of his suffering.

"A robber who thought I'd be no match for him," I answer at last. "He learned his mistake. As will you."

"Andrea, why have you done this?" he asks. "We are *not* married. You're my *patient*, don't you remember?" A silent stretch of time passes as we stare each other in the eyes. "*Please* remember."

"I remember the pain you made me feel when you brought *her* into our lives. We were so happy! Why'd you have to do it? Why'd you have to push me to this? It's your fault, you know. Your fault these two people are dead, and it'll be your own fault when you join them."

KAYLA FREDERICK

"You're delusional," he says and tries to try drag himself toward the stairs.

I decide I like him like this. Alive but incapacitated. This is exactly the level of humiliation I had hoped to see, and it was a stroke of serendipity that brought this to me. I consider keeping him alive for the show. Every time his leg starts to heal, I could break it again. I could break them *both* and watch him suffer endlessly until he wastes away.

That would be so utterly satisfying, but time consuming. I don't know if I'll be able to fly under the radar for as long as that would take. Maybe with a little bit better planning, I could've made it happen, but in *this* reality, I'll have to figure out a different ending for my plaything.

"*I'm* delusional," I laugh and cross the room toward my tools. I can still hear him crawling around behind me, and that makes me only want to laugh harder. "It's just like a man to take a woman for everything, to break her down to her most vulnerable state, then say *she's* the crazy one."

Matthew keeps dragging himself toward the stairs, and I've decided I've had enough. Maybe this show isn't as entertaining as I imagined it would be. I don't care about a slow death now. I want it to be horrific, chaotic, and every bit equal to the emotional pain that this man has forced me to endure. That's when I reach for the chainsaw. I rev it, and it comes to life in my hands.

Matthew pauses briefly at the bottom of the stairs. The pure terror that washes over his face is delicious. If I could harvest it, I would never be sad again. Over the sound of the chainsaw, I barely hear his calls for help which means no one else will either.

MEMENTO MORI

Not that they would've to begin with. This house is so far out in the woods that the nearest neighbor is a decent ten-minute car ride away.

Unlucky for him, I guess.

I approach one slow step at a time, reveling in the look on his face. At one point he tries to frantically pull himself up the stairs as if he thinks he can move faster than me with his femur sticking through his skin.

I don't know what to expect of the chainsaw encountering his flesh. Part of me expects that it'll tear through with ease like my knives, and it does at first. Blood and chunks of flesh fly in every direction, landing on me in a hot spray and painting the walls, stairs, plastic, and dead bodies with his blood. When the chainsaw has cut through the meat to the bone, it stalls, threatening to give up with the blades clogged with meat, but I don't want to stop. And I don't. Not until he's cut in two, a diagonal line across his abdomen from his left shoulder to his right hip.

His face is contorted in pain that stays with him long after his death. I stare directly into his dead eyes and finally switch the chainsaw off, feeling peace for perhaps the first time in my life.

KAYLA FREDERICK

5.

THAT AFTERNOON IS filled with work. Wadding up the plastic sheets and scrubbing every inch of the basement with bleach leaves me a brand-new kind of exhausted. By the time I'm finished with that, the sun is already setting, but I'm nowhere near done. Who knew that murder was such *exercise?*

There are still three bodies in my basement, and I need them gone. I wish I had access to a pig farm. I've heard that a pig can make a grown human disappear in eight minutes. That's much quicker than I can do it. I sit on the bottom of the basement stairs, staring at the three of them.

"What should I do with you?" I ask, eyes running from Katherine, to Morgan, to the pieces of Matthew.

Katherine, being the oldest of the three, is looking the worse for wear. It's nearly been a week now since she died, and the decomposition is kicking in. She stinks, and I take that to be her final *fuck you* to me for having killed her. That's fine. I can handle a little bit of a competition because obviously, I always come out a winner.

I get up, pacing around the room for answers. There's a sledgehammer among Matthew's many tools, and I use that to make a sizable hole in the brick wall. Beyond it, there's a gap. I stick my head inside, hoping I won't run into a bunch of spiders or rats. There's insulation and mildew. It stinks, but what I need this place for stinks more. So in a way, I suppose it evens out.

Body by body, I heave them all inside, still wrapped like big burritos. Matthew is the last one. He's not wrapped up. It

MEMENTO MORI

seems too comfortable to let his body *seem* as if it's still together. I toss the bottom half of him into the room, and he lands beside Morgan. Another toss, and the top half lands by his whore. I scoff. It's like he had wanted in the final moments of his life—to be close to *her*.

Well, now he can be next to her for all of eternity, for all I care.

I toss some of the bloody weapons inside then go to work stacking bricks. I don't have mortar or anything that can make them stay together, and that could be a problem. Some of the bricks are cracked, and that leaves quite a few gaps in the wall. I search through the boxes of supplies in the corner for something to fix it. There has to be *something* here of use. I tear a couple boxes apart before I find a container of silicone.

I flip it over, reading the back. "Extra strength, huh?" I mumble to myself.

It's by no means perfect, but it's better than nothing. I go back to the hole, pushing the bricks out to restart the process, this time adding a thick line between the layers. The finished product is ugly, but it holds together better than the nothing I used on my first attempt. As I stare at it, I'm *almost* proud. On a quick glance, this part of the wall doesn't stand out too much. It's only when someone studies the wall too hard that the irregularities become apparent…or maybe that's because I *know* this is here.

I want the entire *wall* to vanish, but of course, that's not a possibility. *Next best thing,* I think, and turn my attention to a nearby rack. It's heavy, every shelf nearly full of tools, junk, and other random items that people put in storage then forget about completely. At first, I don't think I can move it. There's a pain in my back from all the rigorous activity I've already endured over the past few days, and I'm worried that if I push too hard, that pain will evolve into something serious.

A glance to the wall again has me pushing the pain to the back of my mind as my desperation takes over, lending me a strength I didn't know I had. Inch by inch, I pull the black metal rack to its new place in front of the displaced bricks. It feels like an eternity has passed, and the layer of Matthew's blood that had been on me is joined by dirt, sweat, and grime by the time it's in place in front of the broken wall.

Picking up the discarded items from my glue search, I stack everything onto the empty spaces. The result is a wall completely blocked from sight. Unless anyone decides to move the rack, or the things on it, there's no way to tell that that part of the wall is any different from the rest of them.

Yawning, I roll my shoulders and check for anything else I may have forgotten about. Katherine's purse is still in the tiny nook under the stairs, and I pick it up. Going up the stairs, I calculate my plan for disposing of it. That'll come *after* my shower.

MEMENTO MORI

6.

WHEN I STEP out of the shower, I wipe enough steam off the mirror to see only my eyes. Coming to grips with my new reality will be difficult, but not impossible. I am strong. I am a survivor.

My name is Katherine, and I'm a widow.

KAYLA FREDERICK

MEMENTO MORI

If it is spoken in whispers now, that's because the world has worn out its voice screaming about it in the past.

KAYLA FREDERICK

MEMENTO MORI

Don't Look

I CLUTCHED MY blanket tighter, listening to the scratching at my window. *Screech.* It was the sound of nails on a chalkboard. A chill ran down my spine, and I drew the blanket over my face, ignoring the heat trapped against my skin.

Ignore it... you'll be okay.

That was the strategy I'd used for a week now. Each night, the noises grew louder, and my fear increased with it.

But I was okay.

So far.

Screech, screech. The sounds came faster, as if the creature knew I was weakening, and was desperate to shatter my last bit of courage. Could it smell my fear or was it in tune with its prey's feelings?

I'm too old for this, I thought, burrowing into the pillows.

Was it possible to die of fear?

I didn't know. Against my fear, I tried to go to sleep, but all I could think about was how this had all begun.

With my friend, Bethany.

I'd been on my way to school when she found me. I didn't know that'd be the last time I'd see her. We never really know, do we? I hadn't recognized her at first. She was disheveled—thick, brown, unbrushed hair, heavy bags beneath her eyes, ripped clothes, and worse—a fresh wound on her arm.

"Bethany, oh, my God. What happened? Are you okay?"

I asked, trying to approach her. I felt helpless. She was my best friend, but I hadn't been there to protect her from whatever had caused this.

"Lizey, please. I need…I need you to… listen to me," she said, looking around. "I don't have much time."

"Do we need to go to the police?"

"Whatever you do, don't look at it," she whispered, taking a small step backward. Her gaze was distant, as if she stared into a memory.

"Don't look at what?" I urged, but her movement was becoming quicker, a startled rabbit moving to flee.

Then she did.

"Bethany, wait!" I called and tried to chase her.

It didn't matter how quickly I moved, she was faster. She bounded through the town as if she could go on forever. Inevitably, my energy burned out, and I lost her. I hated myself. My best friend was in trouble, and there wasn't a thing I could do to help her.

That feeling intensified when I found out I was the last person to see her alive.

The police converged at the house two doors down the next day, and I knew that all was not well. I ran outside, joining my neighbors along the edge of the caution tape. Two men wearing coroner's jackets entered the house and came back out with her corpse. My heart sank. I hadn't told anyone about the last time I'd seen her, which I regretted.

I took a few deep breaths, trying to push away those last images of Bethany. Will they find me like that in a few days?

If I don't look, I'll be safe, I tried to convince myself. But was

MEMENTO MORI

I really?

All I had to go by were Bethany's cryptic last words. If it hadn't been enough to save *her*, why would I be any different?

The night the scratching started, I barely lost a wink of sleep. I woke up and went about my routine, but the day had an odd feeling. People barely spoke, and when they did, they were void of emotion. It was like we were all puppets. I didn't want to go to school and see Bethany's desk and locker, but my parents insisted I needed to.

I walked down the hallway, considering ditching for the rest of the day to mourn in peace. Eyes tracked every move I took, and it required a lot of effort to pretend I didn't notice. I opened my locker and nearly dropped my textbook on my toe. A lock of brown hair sat on my shelf, a frilly ribbon tied at one end. Its frayed edges had been dipped in blood, leaving an ugly puddle that stained every book beneath it.

I recognized the hair. It was Bethany's.

Taken after her death, I was sure.

"Who did this?" I yelled at the nearest cluster of my classmates.

No one said a word.

"You think it's funny? She was murdered, you fucks!"

The bell rang, and everyone shuffled past, not bothering to acknowledge me. I felt crazy. *Invisible.* Maybe I was. I sank to the floor, burying my face in my knees for a long time. A light tap on my arm roused me, and sniffling, I glanced up. A teacher stood beside me, offering a gentle smile. I wasn't in any of her classes, so to me, she was a stranger.

"Are you okay?" she asked.

KAYLA FREDERICK

I wiped my eyes and looked at the smear of makeup on my skin. "Yeah, yeah, I'm fine," I squeaked, sticking a cork in the part of me that wanted to spill everything.

She offered another pressed-on smile and said, "Make sure you get to class, okay?"

I nodded, and she walked away. Embarrassed by how many people had seen me at my lowest, I used the mirror on the inside of my locker door to clean my face. Before it closed, I spotted a tiny note sitting beside the lock of hair. My hands shook as I reached for it, eyes on the bloody lock of hair.

I unfolded the paper to find a poem in a cursive script I didn't recognize.

Bethany, Bethany
Why don't you see,
The monster outside
That's coming for me

Chills ran down my spine, and I had the sensation of seeing something I wasn't supposed to. I balled the paper up and tossed it inside the locker, slamming the door. The time would come to deal with what was inside, but today wasn't it. On my walk home, my head reeled with all that had happened.

Who had given Bethany the note? And what did they mean by *the monster*? Did it have to do with Bethany's last words?

I couldn't be sure.

That night, the noises started again. After sleeping through it the first night, I felt annoyed that I was unsuccessful now. I rubbed my eyes before wandering outside to check my window. A broken branch hung lazily from a nearby tree, scraping the glass when the wind blew.

You're just barking in the dark, I told myself and broke the branch, tossing it to the ground.

When I turned to go back inside, my heart plummeted to my stomach. On my windowsill was a lock of brown hair with a bloody ribbon. The exact same one from my locker. My skin prickled with the sensation of being watched, and I ran back inside, barely resisting slamming the door and waking my parents.

How had the lock gotten here? I was sure I'd left it in my locker.

It's a warning, my gut told me.

Whatever you do, don't look at it, Bethany's words echoed in my mind.

My stomach knotted itself into a ball. How could I *not* look if I didn't know what *it* was?

I got back into bed, forcing my eyes to stay closed even when the scratching started again.

HARD TO BELIEVE all this had started only a week ago. It feels like a lifetime has passed. How could I go months like this? Years?

Screech. Screech. SCREECH.

Louder. More desperate. I sobbed silently, holding the blanket tight.

It can't end like this. For Bethany's sake, I can't let it win. I must end it.

Something pounded against the glass, and I bit my tongue, trying not to make a sound. The thuds mimicked the blood pulsing in my ears until the noise I'd been dreading came—the glass shattered, a hailstorm of tiny sparkling shards dusting the floor.

Fear kept me in place, eyes squeezed shut, unsure what to do. Should I make a run for it, or stay under the blanket?

My fear made the choice for me.

"Don't look," I whispered, with shaky breaths. "Don't look."

Floorboards creaked as the creature closed in, pressure on the bed announcing its exact location. It inched closer, and I clasped my hand over my mouth. Tears streamed down my face as fear and adrenaline rushed through my veins. The pressure jumped to my back, and I could imagine a huge grotesque hand wrapping around my midsection like an eagle's talons before sharp pain pierced through my side.

Claws.

I tried to scream, but my throat was so hoarse from crying that I barely made a sound. The creature's other hand grasped the blanket, throwing it aside. Cold air breezed over my face, but I kept my eyes shut, imagining the creature bringing its face close to mine.

It's trying to get your attention, a familiar voice whispered. *It can't hurt you if you refuse to look into its eyes.*

"B-Bethany?" I stammered, feeling the urge to peek in the chance I might catch a glimpse of her.

The claws dug deeper into my skin, tearing through my body like paper. The pain seemed real enough, but I wondered if this was all in my head. A nightmare I hadn't woken from yet.

"Please, please, please," I whispered, though I wasn't sure

MEMENTO MORI

if it was to the creature to release me, or to myself to wake up and pull myself out of this place.

"Run," Bethany whispered, urgently. "Run!"

At the sound of her voice, a dark certainty washed over me that I *wasn't* asleep. My eyes cracked open, picking up the figure of the nightmarish creature hovering over me. Its head swiveled in my direction, large orange eyes pinning my gaze, and I realized too late that I'd made the fatal mistake—I looked.

KAYLA FREDERICK

MEMENTO MORI

Where are the dreamers, the wishers, the believers? If there's no mystery left in the world, we must create our own.

KAYLA FREDERICK

MEMENTO MORI

Stockholm Syndrome

THE HEADACHE IS how I know I'm awake. It's like a pickaxe has been wedged in the middle of my forehead. I groan, struggling to move my fingers. My body comes alive, but it's a slow process. My eyes crack open, and the sharp white light shining down from the ceiling cuts into my vision, intensifying the pain in my brain. As soon as I sit up, nausea washes over me, and I feel for a container, anything I can spew into.

My hand brushes against a metal pan on the floor. I snatch it up and hurl, emptying every meal I've had that day into the silver basin. I choke and at last the stream stops with an awful burning sensation in my chest. I wipe my mouth, hardly able to believe how much liquid came out of me. Disgusted, I set the pan on the floor.

That's when I realize I'm not at home.

I don't know *where* I am.

Glancing down, I study the ugly white gown I'm wearing. It reminds me of hospital attire. A quick look around the room reveals how tiny it is, containing only the bed, the pan, and a toilet.

Am I in prison? I wonder. But that can't be right.

If it's not prison, then where *am* I? How did I get here?

The more I look around, the more confused I become. This isn't like any place I've seen before. The sparkling white walls feed the claustrophobia that has kicked in. My mouth feels dry, made worse by vomiting. How long has it been since I've had something to drink?

"Where am I?" I try to call, but no sound passes my chapped lips.

I swallow, wincing at the slight pain the movement causes, and crawl out of bed. The smooth white tiles feel cool against my bare feet, sending a wave of goosebumps all over my skin. In two steps, I'm at the door. I feel around the edges for a way to pry it open. When that doesn't work, I pound on it, hoping to make enough noise to draw someone's attention.

My voice may fail me, but the sound I make with each strike will not. A slot at the bottom of the door opens, and a tray is shoved through. I spot a container of juice and dive for it, not considering possible ill will. I drain it in four large gulps, relieved. There's a sandwich on the other end of the tray, but I ignore it. After all the vomiting, I don't plan on eating anytime soon.

I toss the empty juice container back onto the tray and push it against the wall, studying the slot it was squeezed through. Using all the strength in my fingertips, I try to push it open, but it won't budge. Sitting back up, I glance at the empty juice container. I should have rationed it better.

Who knows when I'll be given food again?

I try to remember how I got here, but the harder I think, the less I recall. I pace the length of the tiny room, searching for any possible ways to escape. The curls of my brown locks brush against my back with each step I take, the only constant in my life. I don't know what I should do or what I *can* do, really. There seems to be no way out besides the door, and it's stuck shut.

"What is this place?" I call, searching for a camera or

something that could bring me in contact with the people who brought me here, since I'm confident I didn't put myself in this situation.

"Why am I here?" I ask, quieter now.

Silence fills the room again, and I feel that the second question will be ignored like the first. The door clicks then opens. A flare of hope in my chest has me diving toward it, despite my tide of fear. I'm most likely rushing headfirst into danger, but I don't think about it as I peer into the hallway. Nothing's there so I slip out of my room and travel down the corridor.

It's long and clinical, with white walls and light gray tiles that echo my every step. It feels like walking in a nightmare. I turn a corner and voices drift toward me. I'm so happy to not be alone that I start to jog, hopeful that I'll gain some answers or maybe my freedom. That the voices could belong to my kidnappers doesn't occur to me.

The corridor empties into a large white room filled with others dressed in white gowns. I run up to the nearest person, an older woman with salt-and-pepper hair.

"C-can you help me? I've been kidnapped!" I gush. She doesn't answer. Instead, she offers me a wide smile, revealing several broken teeth. A dry, chortling laugh passes through her lips. "We've all been!" she screeches and continues to laugh.

Thrown by the reaction, I back away, glancing at the others. Their faces are blank. Emotionless. I'm under the impression that they're all in the same situation as me, yet they're calm. Have they been drugged?

"I don't understand," I try to tell the woman, when a louder voice overlaps mine, drowning me out.

KAYLA FREDERICK

"Can I get everyone's attention?"

I freeze in the middle of the room, tracing the source of the voice from a door that opened on the other side of the room. A man, about six or seven years older than me, stands there, wearing all white like the rest of us. Something about him is different though, as if he's not here for the same reason the rest of us are.

"I'd like to give a big cheer to Avera, our newest addition!" he says, gesturing to me. I can't think. Everyone in the room looks at me. I feel like I'm on display somehow.

"Newest addition to what?" I ask and try to approach him. If anyone is going to give me answers, he's the best chance I have.

I don't get far before arms snake around my shoulders and a sharp, painful pinch lights up the side of my neck. I go limp, and the white room fades away as I'm dragged down a hallway. I catch eyes with the woman with salt-and-pepper hair before the door slides shut, hiding the room from view.

I come back to consciousness lying on a table. Several shots are injected into my body at different points, and I struggle to move, to fight back, but I've lost control of myself from the neck down. Several times, the blackness swoons up and takes me with it, and each time I come back, I hope to find that the whole thing's been a dream. When I finally come to consciousness for the last time, I'm back in the little room—the prison that had initially greeted me.

I wipe the sweat from my forehead, convinced it was all a bad dream, until I see my bandaged, wrapped arm. I know it's in vain, but still I scream, unable to think of a more productive reaction. I try to get off the bed, but I haven't regained full control from whatever they injected me with. My injured arm collides with the ground first, and I give up my futile attempt at escape, crying myself to sleep in the middle of the floor, but sleep isn't any kinder to me than reality has been.

When I wake, I'm still on the floor, but it's easier to move. I sit up, resting my back against the bed and think back to the white room and all the people I saw in it. Why and how are we here? They were all so calm as they watched me being dragged away. Not a single person tried to help.

You're on your own, I tell myself, glaring at the bandage.

If I want to escape, I have to figure out how to do it alone. I clench my fists, letting the swell of pain from my bandaged arm come and go. Another tray slips through the slot, and I crawl over to it. I gulp down the juice like I had done the day before. Also like the day before, I don't touch the sandwich.

My stomach flips.

It's been at least a day and a half since my last meal but that's not enough to convince me to eat. I stay on the floor, staring at the tray until the door clicks. When it does, I throw myself backward into the wall, afraid of what will come next. Will the men in white storm in to drag me back to their torture chamber?

If they do, I need to fight, I tell myself.

But how?

My mouth fills with saliva, my adrenaline ready for a fight that doesn't come. Like the day before, no one waits in the hallway. On shaky legs, I stand and creep out of the room, following the voices to the big white room. Before I enter it, I backtrack and go the opposite way down the corridor.

It leads to a dead end.

KAYLA FREDERICK

That means the exit must lie in the same hallway as the torture room. With the unsettling feeling of being watched, I walk back down the hallway, past the open door of my prison cell, and into the big white room. Unlike the first day, I study the hallway in detail, noting the locations of the other cells along the way. I peek into one. It's set up the same as mine, right down to the metal pan in the corner.

So why don't the others want to leave? I ask myself.

I stand at the edge of the white room, peering in shyly, like a baby deer. The others are chatting to one another calmly, just like yesterday. About what, I have no idea. They move like peaceful clouds, and I feel oddly at ease as I walk among them. I circle the room once, searching for any weak point I can find. There's a third door in here that I hadn't noticed yesterday. I slink toward it, scared that if I move too fast I'll draw attention to myself.

Could *this* be the way out? I cast a quick glance around before testing it. As suspected, it's locked. I let out a hefty sigh and turn back toward the others, wondering what my next move should be. I do another circle around the room before the familiar booming voice from yesterday calls.

Chills run down my spine, and my arm throbs where they worked on it. I hurry to get to the very center of the group, shrinking inward to blend in with the crowd.

"Miss Rosita, it's your turn," the man announces, flipping through the papers on his clipboard.

"No!" a voice shrieks, slicing through the silence.

I whip around, surprised at the outburst. She's probably a year or two younger than me and struggles as a man in white grabs her and drags her away. She fights back, but they stick a needle in her neck, and she goes limp. I'm desperate to help her, but by the time I reach her, it's too late. The door is sealed shut, and the guard is gone.

"We have to help her!" I holler at the others.

"We *can't* help her," a woman says.

I'm surprised to get a response. More so by the compassion in her eyes. Everyone else does their best to avoid eye contact. I trot up to her. "Why not? Why not fight!? There are more of us than there are of them!"

"It's best to not fight it. They're easier on you if you don't resist," she tells me.

"Wh-what? Who *are* they?" I ask, wanting to know everything about her. How long has she been here? What kind of torture has she endured?

She turns away as if she hasn't heard me. I watch her, disappointed and frustrated. So they're aware they're captives, but they aren't bothered by it.

I purse my lips. *Stockholm Syndrome. They're suffering from Stockholm Syndrome.*

The thought of the months and years this woman might have been contained here makes my skin crawl. What about *my* future? How long do they plan on holding me for, and for what purpose?

What is the point of the experiments?

I don't approach anyone else. I've wasted too much effort on them already. They're too far gone, and I vow to *not* end up like them. I move to the wall and start to pound on the bricks, hoping to find an escape. My goal, useless as it is, helps me keep a tiny bit of sanity.

I alternate taps with glances over my shoulder to the door, waiting for Rosita to come back. I imagine that at this moment, she's being tortured like I'd been the previous day.

I have to know if she's okay.

I walk to the sliding door and run my fingers along its outline, trying to fit into the slot but the space is too thin. I keep trying anyway until my fingertips begin to bleed. Reluctantly, I abandon my mission, resorting to pounding on the door instead.

A red light fills the room, followed by a blaring alarm that assaults my eardrums. I clamp my hands over my ears, surprised to find the others doing the same. At least they're not *completely* unresponsive. The closed door opens, and one of the men who had taken Rosita looks at me.

"Everyone, to your rooms. Now!"

No one protests. They're docile as lambs as they line up to leave the room. But not me. I stand my ground, hands balled into fists at my sides as I confront him.

"Where is she?" I demand. "What have you done to Rosita?"

"It's not your concern," he says, pushing me back.

I will not be swept aside so easily, not without answers. "Tell me, now! You won't get away with this you—"

My insult is interrupted as he grabs my arm and drags me down the hall, past the line of other prisoners. I try to fight, desperate to get away before they can subject me to another torture session, but it doesn't do much. The man's face is stiff as steel, oblivious to my pointless attempts as he thrusts me into my personal Hell and slams the door with a loud clang.

MEMENTO MORI

I jump toward it, but I'm not quick enough to get out. A scream escapes my lips, and I tangle my hands into my hair, sinking to the floor where I rock back and forth in frustration. I can't imagine living the rest of my life in this cell, waiting for my turn to once again undergo their torture.

What will happen to Rosita?

The man had been clean of all traces of blood, but that brings little comfort. My questions remind me of the most important one; the one at the center of this maze.

Why am I here?

Why are any of us here?

What do they want?

I flop over and curl up on the floor, eyes on the slot at the bottom of the door, lost in thought for hours. Finally, I give up and climb onto the bed, staring up at the white ceiling. I try to imagine being here for years. Nothing but white walls and this hard mattress. The smallest tear manages to leak free but stops when I hear a tiny whirring sound.

I freeze, overtaken by uncertainty. Is it coming from something implanted in *me* or something hidden in my room? I pat myself down before I realize that the sound is coming from the furthest corner, beside the metal pan. I clutch the edge of the bed and peer at the floor, trying to pinpoint the source of the noise.

That's when I see it—a mouse.

Creeping easily through a small gap in the wall, it sneaks to the center of the room before it stops short. It senses I'm watching it. Holding my breath, I watch a small antenna sprout from its back with an ugly red light flashing from the tip as if to scan the room. I flinch away, paranoid that it's trying to hurt me. The scan doesn't last long. The antennae snaps back into its body, and I spring at it, trapping the creature under my hands. I pick it up and flip it over. There's a panel with different buttons on it. I poke it, trying to figure out what the buttons do while the mouse's tiny arms and legs flail in its desperate attempt to escape my grasp.

I don't let it go. I can't. I don't know what it is, but I can guess they're using it for surveillance—to monitor the results of their experiments, no doubt. I smile at the mouse, hoping they see the smugness in my eyes before slamming it to the floor, crushing it against the white tile.

Over and over again, I bash it onto the ground until the whirring stops. I stare at the pieces, the mouse's "remains," unsure what to think. I expect someone to show up and scold me for what I've done. But hours pass, and no one does.

Eventually, I crawl back into bed, but I find it nearly impossible to sleep. I keep an eye on the mouse as I toss and turn, certain it will put itself back together and wander off during the night to return its findings. Somehow, I manage to fall asleep, and when I wake, the pieces of the mouse are still there along with a fresh tray of food.

I look between the two, noticing that the other tray is absent. They came into my room again while I was asleep. Had they noticed their device? I laugh to myself, wishing I had stayed awake long enough to see the looks on their faces.

I eat the sandwich today, only because the rumbling in my stomach has become too hard to ignore. A hunger strike isn't the best idea anyway, considering I'll need my strength to fight my way out of here. After breakfast, I pick up every piece of the broken mouse.

I clench my hand shut, the oddly soft pieces poking my palm, and I wait. When the door opens, I run to the white room, pride keeping my head high as I take my place at the center of the room.

"Look! They're watching us!" I shout, holding up the mouse to the others. "They're experimenting on us, and this is how they watch the results! Don't you see we aren't safe here!?" I show the handful of scraps to the nearest woman, but she lifts her nose in disgust.

"Do you all not care?" I ask, shoulders slumping in disbelief. Out of everything I've tried, I was positive *this* would spark some sort of reaction. Instead, they're as deadpanned as ever.

"Avera! What have you got?" the guard calls behind me. I clench my hand around the bits, protective of my find.

"Look! I found your spying equipment. Tell me, what did you do to me that you want to see? Poison? Or did you shoot me up with some rare disease? Some experimental drug?"

"Manny!" he calls over his shoulder. I pull back my arm, intent to throw the mouse at him, but before I have a chance, men in white grab me and pull me down the hall toward the torture room. They strap me to a table, and I fight with everything I can, ready for the torture to begin.

Everything goes black.

When I wake again, I'm back in my room with another pounding migraine. I stare up at the ceiling, tears in my eyes. I suddenly understand the others, their lack of desire to escape.

Maybe at one point they'd been like me, but they hit a wall and ultimately came to the same conclusion—leaving is impossible.

It's best to not fight it. They're easier on you if you don't resist.

When the door opens, I don't notice. I stay in my pit of agony and despair.

"*Psst!*" a sharp whisper startles me back to the present.

Fight or flight kicks in, and I bolt upright, only to see Rosita peeking in at me. She's battered and bruised, and I can only imagine the horrors she's gone through. Deep purple bags sit under her eyes, and her curly brown hair is wild. It looks like some of it has been torn out.

"What happened to you?" I manage to ask, despite the nagging dryness in my throat. There's a tray with a fresh round of food, and Rosita hands me the juice box.

"The same thing that happens to us all, I imagine," she says.

I force myself to my feet, understanding that she's probably as uncomfortable as I am with sharing the details of our torture.

"Why are you here?" I ask instead.

She ignores the question. "You want to escape too," she says, running her tongue nervously over her bottom lip, "and you seem to be the only one."

That gets my attention. I see the desperation in her eyes, the very same that lives inside of me. She hasn't been broken yet either. "You have a plan?"

She glances over her shoulder into the hallway, most likely paranoid that she's being watched, before she takes a step closer to me, the wildness glowing in her eyes. "They let their guard down around the others because they know they won't fight them."

"Yeah, and?"

"We can use that to our advantage. All we need is a distraction. If we get that needle before we get poked, we can use it on him and get down that hallway before the others realize what's happened."

"You're sure the way out is down that way?" I ask. "What about the other door?"

"I don't know," she admits, "but I'm willing to risk it."

At this point, I'm ready to risk it too. She's probably God's answer to the prayers I sent the other day, and I don't want to fumble it.

"Follow my lead, okay?" she says.

She really is a Godsend, I think, following her into the hallway.

My heart pounds in anticipation. We're really doing this. We're really going to be free. She picks up the pace, putting a bit of distance between us. I hold back, waiting for her to enter the white room first. I'm a few seconds behind her, and I stick close to the wall, not so much as glancing in her direction for fear of raising suspicion. I blend among the others, waiting for a signal. There's a clattering sound, and she cries out.

"My leg! I think there's something wrong with my leg!"

I finally risk a glance her way, and see she's collapsed on the floor, coddling her left knee. The guard rushes to kneel beside her, searching her over for some sign of injury.

"Are you alright?"

We make eye contact for a fraction of a second. My cue. I

rush forward, but the guard turns at the sound of my footsteps. He stands to grab my arm but stops before he makes contact. I take an uncertain half step backward, and he collapses to the ground.

    Rosita tosses the needle next to him, and I help her stand before we dash down the unguarded hallway. Shouts come from behind us, but we ignore it, knowing if we fail this time, we most likely won't have another opportunity. Now, I pray that Rosita was right about the location of the exit. I can't bear to think about the consequences if she's wrong.

    Rosita is more athletically fit than I am and keeps the same pace even when I start to lag behind. She hits the door first and rushes through it. Fresh air drifts in, and I take a giant lungful as my bare feet pound the cement. We're in a parking lot, the stones hot beneath our feet. The sunlight is enough encouragement to ignore the pain and keep going.

    All I think about is freedom.

"AND THAT'S WHEN you went to the police, correct?" the prosecutor asks.

    I nod.

    "No more questions."

    "The witness may step down while the jury goes into deliberation," the judge says, banging his gavel.

    Relief swells in my chest as I cross the courtroom to sit beside Rosita. In her suit, she looks much more put together than the first time I'd seen her. Less than an hour later, the jury takes their seats. The judge lumbers back to his spot.

MEMENTO MORI

"Has the jury reached a verdict?"

"We have, your honor," the foreman replies. I hold my breath.

"For the crime of kidnapping, we find the defendant… guilty. For the charge of assault, we find the defendant… guilty. For the charge of unlawful imprisonment, we find the defendant… guilty."

"Guilty!" I whisper. "Guilty!"

I try to look at Rosita, but the courtroom blurs to blackness.

"HOW ARE YOU feeling today, Miss?" a voice asks.

I struggle to open my eyes, and when I succeed, all I see is white. I don't understand. Am I in the room again? I squint to see the tiny woman beside me.

A nurse.

"Looks like someone's stopped taking her medicine!" she says, handing me a cup of water.

I sip the clear liquid, swallowing a handful of colorful pills with it, and notice the bandages around my wrists, cloths protecting the stitches in my self-inflicted wounds. The metallic water brings clarity with it, and I suddenly remember where I am.

I'm in Brentwood Psychiatric.

KAYLA FREDERICK

MEMENTO MORI

Whisk me away from the pain of the night, the darkness of myself, and the horror of my mind. Breathe for me when I am no longer capable of doing so.

KAYLA FREDERICK

MEMENTO MORI

Dreamcatcher

THERE'S SOMETHING TO be said for when the weather outside is nearly perfect yet a storm rages in your mind.

I brush a stray tear from the corner of my eye, feeling how puffy and swollen the skin has become and wish I would've brought my sunglasses. Sniffling, I wipe my nose on the back of my hand. Under any other circumstances, that would seem disgusting, but no one says a word. It's almost as if they expected my manners to go out the window.

I'm surrounded by people, but it's easy to pretend that I'm alone, just me in this sea of grass, watching the open grave not twenty feet ahead of me. I look up at the sky, at the seemingly cheerful sun. It's a horrific reminder that the world won't stop spinning.

Only mine has.

Oddly enough, this same day that's brought me such darkness might be the best day of someone else's life. After what happened to my mother? Anything is possible.

I pick a piece of lint off my black sleeve and adjust the rose between my fingers. Small but normal actions to get me through this unordinary day. Each of the rose's petals seem to take on a different color. That's one result of working with hybrids. Botany usually brings me a sense of peace and joy, but not today. Gazing at my mother's coffin lying a few feet away is a sobering reminder that this "new" thing is now my life. I can't go back to how things used to be.

Beside me, my best friend, Carson, dips his head to catch my eyes. "Are you in there, Evie?"

I twirl the rose but say nothing. What's there to say, after all? Carson pulls his lips into a thin, tight line before pushing my charcoal black hair aside. "You're tough, I get it," he says and wipes a stray tear off my face.

I nod. It's a lame way to converse, but I want him to know I've heard him and that his words keep me going. Without his optimism, I'd be left solely to the shadows. I hardly feel the tips of his fingers dig into my elbow as he pulls me away from the scene, but I don't protest. I don't have it in me. My mother's coffin looms at the forefront of my brain. Even when it isn't directly in front of me, it's all I can see.

When I blink, it's gone, replaced by her bloody, broken body on the bathroom floor. I force the images away and come to in the passenger seat of Carson's car. He gives me a sideways glance through wisps of blond hair, but it takes me a full minute to realize I'm crying. The water feels ridiculously warm on my skin, and I move so fast to wipe it away that I nearly smack myself in the face.

"It's okay, Evie," he assures me as another tear breaks free.

This time, I let it go. He's right. Why am I fighting? My mom just committed suicide, yet I'm more worried about what people will think.

I disgust myself sometimes, I do. "Where are we going?" I ask, my voice sounding raspy. My throat is so dry it hurts.

MEMENTO MORI

"I already know what you're going to say, but I feel like we could both use some food in our stomachs."

"But I'm not hungry," I protest.

Carson shakes his head. "You've got to eat, Evie. You need to take care of yourself."

Frowning, I rest my cheek on the window, mind far too shot to argue. I watch the passing buildings and plants as we leave the city limits, recognizing the dirt path that leads to Carson's house.

"Daniel's here today," he says as the car comes to a halt.

"Okay," I say, slumping farther down in my seat. Daniel has never been my favorite person, but he *is* Carson's brother, and for that reason only, I deal with him rain or shine.

I follow Carson into the house. He disappears into the kitchen, leaving me to stand awkwardly by myself in the living room. I tug my sleeves down over my wrists before I sit on the couch. Pots and pans clang as Carson moves around the kitchen, throwing something together for lunch.

As soon I begin to relax, I hear footsteps on the stairs, and a thousand emotions wash over me. By the time Daniel comes around the wall and into the living room, I'm prepared.

"Hello," I say curtly, eyes on the television across the room.

"Woo, girl, you look like hell," he says, not breaking stride as he joins Carson in the kitchen.

A tear slips from my eye, but I hardly notice it as I glare at Daniel's short blonde hair. "Yeah, just got to it."

He pauses and glances over his shoulder. "What's up your ass today?"

KAYLA FREDERICK

"Hey, man, chill," Carson says, appearing in the living room. He whispers something in his brother's ear. I know what he told him, but Daniel's expression doesn't change. "Sucks," he says, disappearing into the kitchen, leaving Carson with an apologetic look on his face.

"Sorry," he says. "Food's almost ready," he offers as an afterthought, before following his brother out of the room.

I'm almost grateful for the anger Daniel has caused me. It's a distraction, a vital ruse to keep me away from the biting pain deep inside. The more I focus on his snippy comments, the easier it is to forget, for a while, where I had come from, and why I'm here to begin with.

Daniel strolls back through the living room and toward the stairs, clutching a beer in his hand. He pauses at the edge of the room. I narrow my eyes, pretending to watch television and ignore him.

"Hey," he says.

"Yes?" I say through gritted teeth but refuse to look his way.

"I know it hurts, but keep your head up, okay? You'll be fine," he says. The sound of his footsteps on the stairs marks his departure. I stare at the spot where he'd been standing, shocked. Those were the nicest words he's ever said to me, and I'm not sure what to do with them. I don't have much time to decide before Carson comes back into the room, carrying a plate of spaghetti and a cup of tea.

"Eat, please," he says, pulling out a T.V. tray to set them on.

I stare at the food, still not hungry. "Thank you," I say

MEMENTO MORI

anyway. I feel bad rejecting his generosity, so I pick up the fork and stir the pasta around, pretending to eat.

That seems to satisfy him. We fall silent, watching television, and occasionally hear Daniel stomping around upstairs. I don't eat, and Carson pretends not to notice. Less than an hour later, he cleans up the dishes and we're back on the road again. Outside the window, the world rushes past, offering a temporary distraction. That's when I see a sign made of aged wood with sloppy red paint smeared on it.

"Handmade dreamcatchers," Carson and I echo one another.

"Your mom liked that kind of stuff, didn't she?" he asks.

Dreamcatchers, wolves, eagles, anything remotely spiritual. "Yeah, she loved them." I think of the ornate one she'd painted on the living room ceiling. She believed in bad luck and karma. I think the dreamcatchers made her feel safe. Whenever she'd have a particularly bad spout of anxiety or depression, she believed they would take her pain for her.

I never had the heart to tell her otherwise.

Carson flicks on his turn signal, oblivious to the memories flitting through my mind.

"Where are we going?" I ask, with the smallest snivel.

"We're going to see what those dreamcatchers look like."

That brings a smile to my face.

***

THE ADDRESS ON the sign leads us down an old road people stopped using years ago. I have my reservations, but Carson doesn't show a hint of worry. Sunlight bleeds through the trees as he continues onward, as confident as he'd been an hour before. We finally arrive at a rundown home that resembles a shack more than a house. I can nearly smell the decay.

A shiver passes down my spine, and I can't imagine going inside. "Are you sure about this, Carson?"

He squeezes my knee, then climbs out. Not wanting to be left alone, I follow him. We stir up dust on the way to the door and the grit fills my nose, causing me to sneeze. Carson reaches the door first and knocks. It cracks open, and an old man peers out at us. An eerie smile lights his face, showing all his yellow, broken teeth. The man is frail, but that doesn't help the uneasy feeling in my stomach. His face scrunches, thick bushy eyebrows obscuring his beady eyes.

"Hello, sir," Carson greets, polite as ever, and I doubt he got the same creepy vibe from this man that I did. "We saw your sign for dreamcatchers?"

The man's smile grows wider, and he steps aside, opening the door to its full extent. "Ah, yes. Come right in." His gaze lands on me, and he pauses. "Have I seen you before?"

I scrunch my face and shake my head.

"Huh," he says and disappears inside.

Carson takes a step to follow him, but I grab his hand, stopping him. I want to tell him to turn around, to forget it, that there's something off about this whole thing, but the words lodge in my throat.

Maybe it's all in my head.

"Come on," he says.

Unsure what to do, I follow.

MEMENTO MORI

The inside of the shack is as bad as the outside. It stinks. I don't know if the smell is coming from the moldy dishes in the sink or the general decay of the building itself, but all I want to do is get far away from it.

"I have quite a few dreamcatchers on hand," the man says, stopping beside a table in the middle of the room.

I jump at the sound of his voice, almost forgetting the reason for our arrival. "I'm sorry, I don't think I caught your name," I say to the man.

"My name is irrelevant, my art speaks for itself," he replies.

Strange.

Carson and I look at each other, then the table.

Carson's uneasiness fades when he sees the dreamcatchers. "Evie…Evie, look! These are beautiful!"

He's right, of course. They're the most beautiful pieces of art I've ever seen. One is emerald, my favorite color. All my reservations leave as I run my fingers over the threads, thinking about how much I want to own one.

"How much?" Carson asks, pulling his wallet from his back pocket.

Next thing I know, we're sitting in the car with the dreamcatcher in my hands. I try to remember how Carson got me out of the house and how I blacked out at the part where he paid, but I'm at a loss. When my eyes land on the dreamcatcher, all other thoughts move to the back of my mind. I'm drawn to it, but I can't figure out why. Tracing the lines of the web, I hardly notice when the car pulls to a stop.

"Are you gonna be okay by yourself?" Carson asks.

KAYLA FREDERICK

I realize we're outside of my house. Dazed, I nod. "I'll manage, Carson. Thank you so much."

"Anytime, Evie. I'll stop by tonight after work to check on you," he says, pulling me into one of the tightest hugs of my life. I savor it and climb out of the car, too preoccupied with the precious bundle in my hands to focus on much else.

I cross through the living room. Mom had it heavily decorated with wolf figurines and intricate tapestries depicting forests and moons. A purple dreamcatcher hangs from one wall, dwarfed by the giant one she had painted on the ceiling.

As I trudge to my room, I brainstorm possible places to hang my new possession. The poster above my bed has to go. Quick work is made of tearing it down and replacing it with my new prize. I don't know how long I stand there, admiring the green against the gold wallpaper, but before I know it, I'm tired. I can barely keep my heavy eyelids open, so I crawl into bed. The last image I see before slipping into unconsciousness is the eye of the dreamcatcher.

The dream I find myself in is cold and dark. A steady drip of water sounds from somewhere far away. I assume I'm in a cave. Desperate to maintain a bit of warmth, I fold my arms across my body, trying to figure out how I got here. I remember falling asleep, but this doesn't *feel* like a dream. It's too vivid. Footsteps echo in the darkness, and I freeze, glancing over my shoulder. Wherever *here* is, I'm not alone. I take two steps deeper into the cave, the earth chilling my bare feet.

Dread creeps up my spine with icy fingers, colder than the rocks. I bolt through the darkness, snarls and footsteps not too far behind. It doesn't take long for me to tire, desperate for rest I can't afford. My foot slides, and I scream for help that won't come. The sound echoes upward as my body falls. At this moment, so dangerously close to death, it's hard to remember that I'm alone.

***

CARSON'S BROW CRINKLES as he stares at the red light hanging at the last intersection before Evie's house, trying to will it to change. He couldn't stop thinking about her and felt terrible leaving her alone so soon after her awful discovery. He hates his worthless 9-to-5 job more than ever for preventing him from having one day off to be with his childhood friend.

    He glances at his phone on the passenger seat beside him, waiting for the screen to light up with a text from Evie. He hadn't heard from her yet—not so much as a simple one-word answer to any of his messages—and it worries him. When the light turns green, Carson floors it, despite angry honks from the cars around him.

    Carson pulls up in front of Evie's house and kills the engine. The place is dark, causing his brow to furrow in concern. Something's not right, his instinct warns, but his logic argues back.

    Maybe she's asleep.

    He pushes his worries aside and heads into the blackness of the house. It's harder to see inside. Digging his phone out of his pocket, he shines the light ahead of him and makes it through the hallway. At the base of the stairs, the light dims, then goes out completely.

    "Come on," he groans, smacking his phone. The light

stays off. "Damn it," he mutters, slipping the useless thing back into his pocket.

His eyes had adjusted to the bit of light, so now he's even less aware of where he is. His fingers glide against the wall as he makes his way to Evie's room.

"Evie!" he calls.

No response.

As soon as he steps into her room, the electricity blares to life, the sudden brightness blinding him. Then he starts to make out the scene before him. Some sights are so horrific the brain can't comprehend them, so a person will keep staring, hoping it'll all make sense. The feeling eats every inch of Carson's body as his eyes trail from the bloodstains on the white carpet to the cold body lying on the bed.

Silver glints from her bloody hand. A knife or a piece of a broken mirror? He can't say for sure. Tears stream down Carson's face as he forces himself to tear his eyes from Evie's body. Only then does he notice a beautiful purple dreamcatcher—identical to the one he'd bought—hanging beside her green one.

MEMENTO MORI

When we glance in the mirror, do we really see ourselves or a reflection of who we believe ourselves to be?

KAYLA FREDERICK

MEMENTO MORI

Mirror Image

1.

THE HOUSE WAS a great Victorian beauty with wide windows and a wraparound porch. The roof slanted between the two floors, giving it a Gothic edge made complete by the dark siding and shutters.

Olivia couldn't stop running her eyes over its every feature. It was more beautiful than the online listing had shown. That was a welcome relief. Pictures could only show so much. She'd been hesitant about shopping for a new home with no way to see it in person before any final decisions were made.

Cautiously, she glanced at her boyfriend, Clayton, beside her. His golden hair reflected the afternoon sun, and he was grinning in that easy carefree way she loved. Based on his expression now, she never would've guessed he'd been less than keen for this only a few days prior. Not that she could blame him. If things had been reversed, Olivia probably would've felt that same spark of hesitation. After all, this entire move was for her. After being contacted by a headhunter for the top psychology office in the city, she couldn't say no.

The downside was the abrupt cross-country move.

"What do you think?" Olivia asked.

Clayton was silent for a full minute before he said, "I love it."

Olivia turned to him with stars in her eyes. In general, she liked to think of herself as a cheery person, but she'd never felt such *joy*, such completeness. This was like a scene out of one of her favorite romcoms. "You mean it?"

"I do," he said, wrapping her in a hug. "I know I haven't been very supportive of this so far, but that's going to change, okay? This is going to be great."

Olivia couldn't agree more.

The rumble of tires on gravel sounded from the road as the moving truck wove its way up the path.

"Finally," Clayton said, pecking Olivia on the lips. "I'm gonna help them start bringing stuff in."

"I'll come too," she said.

He shook his head. "You've got a full day ahead of you tomorrow. You don't need to be sore for that."

"Are you sure?" she asked.

"Positive. Go explore. Enjoy yourself," he said and reached out to tuck a strand of her red hair behind her ear. "Consider this my way of making things up to you."

Olivia puffed out her cheeks, relieved. Packing all the boxes had been its own feat and so would unpacking. "Okay. I can work with that."

Clayton offered another smile and jogged to the truck, calling to the men climbing out. Olivia studied the outside of the house again. Sure, it had exceeded her expectations, but she wouldn't feel completely satisfied until she explored the inside as well. Olivia stepped through the front door, admiring the stained-glass windowpanes on either side.

Eyes wide, she looked up at the parlor ceiling, before

going through a walkway that led to what she guessed to be the kitchen. On the other side was a staircase. With easy steps, she walked through the ornate dining room and into the pantry before her wanderings took her up the staircase.

Her fingers trailed the hand carved wooden banister, and when her feet stepped onto the landing, her jaw gaped open. Like the parlor, the upstairs had an airy feel. A red plush carpet lined the hall all the way down to the wall at the end. From where she stood, she could see the window beyond the white curtain.

Olivia strode down the hall, confident as she peered into each door she passed. At last, she made it to the window and noticed a string dangling from the ceiling. Knitting her eyebrows together, she followed it upward.

An attic. It led to an attic.

The ad said nothing about an attic.

However, it made sense that a house as old as this one would have one. She reached up to pull the ladder down, expecting it to stick. It came down easily as if it had been recently oiled. *Why wouldn't they mention this?*

The ladder led up to blackness, and she had a moment of internal debate. Who knew the last time someone had been up there? It could be full of spiders or snakes or any type of vermin. It might not be structurally safe either. Olivia moved to close the panel, convinced she'd explore when Clayton was ready to join her. Except if she did that, she'd most likely have to wait until tomorrow or the day after that.

By and large, Olivia was not a patient person.

Hand over hand she climbed, blackness engulfing her. She had the afterthought of bringing a flashlight, but she was already up the ladder. A pullcord brushed across the top of her head, and she yanked it, not expecting the light to work, but it did. A mass of shapes covered in white sheets lined the walls. Light dustings of cobwebs sprinkled the boards overhead. The air was musty and thick as if the attic hadn't gotten a fresh supply in some time.

    Olivia took it all in. Cautiously, she lifted the covering from the closest shape, revealing a statue underneath. It was a woman with thin, wiry arms and a billowy dress. The white marble eyes stared straight ahead into nothingness. Intrigued, Olivia pulled another tarp to the side, this time revealing a delicate painting of roses. The more tarps she removed, the more pieces of artwork she encountered. There had to be at least a hundred of them in total.

    Maybe more than that.

    This didn't look like an attic in a two-hundred-year-old house. It was as if someone had left an entire art museum crammed up here and forgotten about it. She bent down to run her fingers over the intricate engravings on the lip of a vase, and her eyes dropped to a shape hidden beneath the easel of one of the paintings. It was square, covered in a white sheet, held tightly in place by thick bands of silvery tape. Olivia expected it to be another painting, and took a step forward, ready to investigate when Clayton's voice stopped her.

    "Olivia!" he called from somewhere in the house.

    She made a move toward the stairs when the statue she had first seen caught her eye. The arm was up, one delicate finger pointing to the wrapped bundle.

    Had it been like that earlier? Olivia couldn't remember.

    "Olivia!" Clayton called again.

MEMENTO MORI

    Olivia scrutinized it one more time before descending the ladder back into the house.

KAYLA FREDERICK

2.

DESPITE CLAYTON'S PROTESTS, Olivia did what she could to help unload the rest of the truck. By the time nightfall came, they were sweaty and exhausted, but they managed to get all their belongings into the house. The next few days would oversee them putting it all away, but for the time being, they were content to rest.

Since the stove wasn't hooked up yet, Clayton ordered pizza. When they sat down to eat, Olivia remembered the attic and her discovery.

She set her piece of pizza down onto her flimsy paper plate, staring at the grease stains. "Did you know we had an attic?"

"An attic?" Clayton echoed through a mouthful of food.

"Yeah. I think an art dealer used to live here or something. Lots of statues and paintings. Kind of dusty, but for the most part, they're all in good shape."

"Cool. Maybe some of them are worth something," Clayton said and popped the rest of his slice into his mouth. "I'll check it out in the morning."

"Yeah, maybe," Olivia said, thinking that she would contact Renee, their realtor, as soon as she could to inquire about the previous resident. It didn't seem right to sell them without at least trying to contact the owner first.

They didn't talk more about the attic as they went through their nightly routine. As Olivia lay in Clayton's arms that night, she was once again faced with the dilemma of what she thought she'd seen. The statue. The arm that moved. For as crazy as it sounded, she was sure that was exactly what had happened.

When sleep finally claimed her, she opened her eyes to the attic. Darkness. Then a flash of red. The statues turned toward her. Another flash. They moved closer. She was surrounded by them, the square bundle held toward her in their plastic fingers.

She gasped and slammed back into consciousness so suddenly that it took her a full minute to realize she wasn't in the dream anymore. Olivia reached out toward Clayton's side of the bed, petting the cold fabric. He wasn't beside her. It was unusual for Clayton to wake before her, but she supposed it wasn't unheard of. She thanked the stress of the move for it. In fact, she was surprised she had gotten any sleep at all.

Olivia sat up, scanning the room. The light was off in the bathroom. "Clayton?"

No response.

She got out of bed, peering down the hall. A quick walkthrough showed he wasn't in the kitchen either. She ascended the stairs, and that was when she saw light at the end of the hall. The attic's silver ladder hung down, inviting her up.

"Clayton, you up here?" she called as she began to climb.

"Yeah."

Clayton sat cross-legged on the floor. The lump Olivia had left carefully bundled sat before him except he'd taken off the sheet to reveal a mirror. It was set in a frame with an intricate red base carved into a dragon. On one side of the mirror was the dragon's face and the other, its tail. Compared to the vibe of the rest of the pieces, it was almost...*jarring*.

"Isn't it beautiful?" Clayton asked, running his finger over the engraved scales down the dragon's back.

"It is," Olivia said, though that wasn't her original thought.

The mirror left her uneasy.

"We should bring it downstairs," Clayton said with puppy-dog eyes.

Usually, that was all it took for him to get his way, regardless of the argument at hand, but she *really* didn't want to bring the mirror downstairs. She wanted to put the sheet back on it and hide it away.

"Let's leave it up here for now," Olivia said. Clayton wilted, and she added, "At least until we unpack. That way we won't accidentally knock it over. It'd be a uh…shame to break something so beautiful."

Clayton didn't look so warm anymore, but he didn't argue. He stood up, giving the mirror one long last glance, as if he were saying goodbye to an old friend, before he turned back to her.

"Let's go get breakfast."

MEMENTO MORI

3.

THE MORNING'S EVENTS had left Olivia unsettled, but breakfast fixed any weirdness between her and Clayton. She felt better as she got dressed, and she wasn't worried about anything but making a good first impression. Last night, she'd been so bothered by the attic that it hadn't hit her how big of a day it was.

Clayton kissed her and wished her good luck before she walked down the driveway to the car. She slipped into the seat and sat there, staring at the steering wheel.

I can do this, she told herself, but she didn't feel it.

Part of her was still focused on Clayton in the attic. How *wrong* his eyes had looked when she'd told him to leave the mirror in the attic.

I'm imagining things, she thought and put the key in the ignition. *Just like the statue.* Stress was excellent for making someone see the worst in nothing. She knew that from experience.

As she drove, her finger rhythmically tapped on the steering wheel to the music. "Call Renee."

Her music was replaced with a dial tone, and Olivia bit her knuckle as she waited for the call to connect. When Renee's voicemail picked up, Olivia was a mix of frustrated and relieved. She hadn't been sure what she would say anyway and disconnected the call without leaving a message. Hopefully, by the time Renee called her back, she'd have a better idea of what she would ask.

***

KAYLA FREDERICK

THE DAY WENT smoother than she'd anticipated. Between the new faces and things to do, Olivia had very little time to fret over her new home. In fact, she was so busy she forgot about her worries completely. When she left work for the day, she had a giant smile on her face and couldn't wait to see Clayton to tell him every minute of her day.

It dropped the second she walked through the door. The big ugly mirror was on the table by the staircase. To come or go from the house meant walking past it. Olivia shuddered. Then her eyes went to Clayton. He was bent in front of it, staring at himself as if he couldn't get enough of his reflection. When she closed the door with a thud, he didn't look away.

"You…brought it down," she said with an uncertain laugh.

"I did," Clayton replied. There was a flash of something in his eyes. Something she couldn't quite recognize. He hid it with a smile. "Do you like it?"

She *hated* it and the feeling of dread that came with it. The more she protested, the more he'd fight her about it. After all he'd done for her, she should be willing to give in, willing to give him his way to keep the peace, but Olivia was unable to shake the feeling that there was something wrong with the mirror. Somehow, she pushed it all down. In a few weeks, she was sure he'd lose interest in it, and she'd move it back to the attic if she didn't chuck it directly in the trash.

MEMENTO MORI

4.

THAT NIGHT, SLEEP didn't come easily, and when Olivia woke up, Clayton was once again not in bed. It didn't take long to find him in the parlor, crouched before the mirror. From where she stood, it almost seemed as if Clayton were attempting to crawl directly through the shiny surface. Two candles sat on either side of the red frame, the light reflecting in a way that gave him inhuman eeriness.

"What are you doing up?" she asked, fingers gripping the doorframe beside her. It was then she realized she was *afraid* of this. Afraid of Clayton.

Clayton didn't look at her, and she wondered if she'd spoken out loud.

Olivia drew her eyebrows together and took a step closer. "Clayton, did you hear me?"

Slowly, his head cocked to the side, focus still on the mirror.

"Clayton." She paused to clench her hands into fists. "What are you doing?"

Clayton continued to ignore her, and Olivia started to grow angry. It was one thing to move around the furniture to his liking, but something else entirely to ignore her.

"*Clayton*!" she nearly hollered. "This is weird. What in the world are you doing?"

No response.

Olivia had had enough. "I don't know what this is, but I'm over it. I'm putting this mirror back up in the attic for now, and we can talk about it in the morning."

Clayton went rigid as Olivia approached. Before her fingers grazed the red frame, he snatched her wrist in a grip so tight she could nearly *feel* her bones grinding together.

"You're not taking it *anywhere*," he hissed, anger radiating from him.

She'd seen him mad before, of course, but she'd never seen Clayton like *this*. She tried to pull her arm free, but he didn't let go. He advanced toward her, pupils so blown his eyes appeared black.

"You're hurting me," she whimpered.

Clayton's grip tightened and spit droplets rained on her face as he said, "Don't ever touch the mirror."

Olivia had never felt such fear before. She cowered, hoping he would snap out of it, but before she could say or do anything else, he flung her away. She slammed into the wall with a heavy thud. Pain shot through her elbow and hip from the point of contact, but she hardly noticed as she watched Clayton move for the door. It slammed shut behind him, and Olivia struggled to process what had happened.

"Clayton!" she called.

He was gone.

She took a few steps into the yard, head swiveling back and forth, but she didn't see him. Their car was still in the driveway, and Olivia couldn't understand what had happened. She hadn't given him that much of a head start. There should be some sign of where he'd gone.

"Clayton!"

No response.

Sniffling, she took a step backward and hurried into the house, down the hall to their room. With shaking fingers, she scooped her phone up off the bedside table and dialed Clayton's number. It rang and rang before his voicemail picked up.

"It's Clayton. Can't answer right now but drop a message. I'll call back."

It beeped, and Olivia launched into her message. "Clayton! Where are you? What's going on? Please call me back, or better yet, *come home!*"

With shaking fingers, she set it down, and her eyes went to the red ring of fingerprints around her wrist. Clayton had never hurt her before, and she couldn't understand why he would now.

It's the mirror, a hypnotic voice whispered in her ear. *He looked into the mirror, and now it's got him.*

Olivia shook her head. It was insanity. And like the very definition, she found herself calling him once again.

"It's Clayton. Can't answer right now but drop a message. I'll call back."

"Please come back," she whispered and hung up.

OLIVIA SPENT THE next few hours pacing and dialing Clayton's phone. She heard nothing back. Dread settled in her gut the same way it had the first time she'd seen the mirror. She didn't want to believe it had anything to do with Clayton's behavior, but she couldn't avoid the thought either. Each round of pacing brought her closer and closer to the ugly thing. So much time had passed since Clayton stormed out that the candles on either side had burned out. It didn't make the scene any less haunting. When she closed her eyes, she could still see the darkness of his eyes, the *hatred,* as he'd approached her.

When the first rays of morning sun shone through the stained-glass windows, a flash of red and blue lights came with them.

Cop cars.

"Uh-oh," Olivia said and worked up the nerve to hurry past the mirror.

A feeling in her gut told her that Clayton had done *something.* If he was in jail, it certainly explained why he hadn't come home. She whipped open the door before anyone could knock, desperate to see what they had to say.

When the approaching officer saw her, he took off his hat. "Miss Olivia Garcia?"

"That's me," she said, clutching onto the door frame with a sickening feeling of foreboding in her gut.

"I'm sorry to say there's been an accident."

MEMENTO MORI

5.

DEAD.

Clayton was dead.

Olivia spent the entire afternoon sitting at the kitchen table, staring at her hands. She was in shock. She knew that, but she didn't know how to break herself out of it. Just as she didn't know how she got through the rest of that day. The officer had taken her to the morgue to identify the body. The room was so cold and white she could imagine it was what death itself was like. They pulled a silvery tray out of a cabinet. A bundle of gore had been covered only by a thin sheet.

They'd needed her to make a positive ID, but she could barely tell that the mass of tissue had at one time been human, let alone a human she had loved. A few of his belongings had been scattered in the road and those were the ultimate decision makers. It was also how the cops had known to find her.

The rest of the day passed in a fog, and the next thing she knew, it was morning, she was home, and she was alone. Closing her misty eyes, her head filled with everything the officer had told her. Clayton had run into a busy freeway and been hit by a semitruck. They ruled it suicide, but Olivia wasn't ready to accept that. Clayton had never been the suicidal type. Nor had he ever been violent.

The mirror, the voice whispered again. *It was the mirror.*

Olivia's cellphone started to ring. She jumped and grabbed it off her end table. Renee was calling back. Olivia sniffled. Her questions about the art in the attic seemed like a memory from years prior rather than a few days.

"Hello, Renee," Olivia said, trying to sound as polite as she could, given the circumstances.

"Olivia, dear," Renee said. "I'm so sorry I couldn't get back to you the other day. I was busy, busy. But I wanted to touch base with you today. Is everything alright?"

Olivia smiled bitterly, twin tears leaking from either eye. Of course everything was *not* alright, but she didn't have it in her to get into it. "The house is wonderful," Olivia forced out, trying to choke back the sob that wanted to accompany it. "I wanted to ask you about the previous resident."

"What about him, hon?"

"Did something…happen to him? I found an attic filled with all kinds of artwork. I wasn't sure what to do with it. It seems wrong to get rid of it all. Is there a forwarding address or something so I can get in contact with him?"

Renee was silent, and Olivia held the phone from her face, checking to see if the call was still active.

"I'm sorry to say there's no way to reach him," Renee said.

Olivia held her hand up. "Is he…"

"Dead? Oh, Lord only knows. He disappeared around the start of the year. No one has heard anything since. As far as the artwork goes, it, along with everything else, was foreclosed with the house. It's technically yours now."

"Oh," Olivia said, feeling only worse for the knowledge.

"You're sure everything is okay?"

Olivia hung up, no longer having the desire to be polite. The thoughts swirling in her head made her sick, and she held a hand to her forehead to steady herself. The previous resident was missing.

Clayton was dead.

Maybe most troubling of all, that damn mirror was now hers.

Olivia grabbed her phone and pulled up the search bar. She typed in her address, scrolling through the first few listings of ads that Renee hadn't taken down yet. Toward the bottom of the first page was an article.

Local man missing.

Olivia clicked it, already knowing what it would say. It gave little more on his situation than Renee had. The difference was the picture. A smiling man stared back at her, the word *missing* written in red beneath it.

Shivering, Olivia clicked off the phone and slammed it to the table as she rose to her feet, thinking longingly of her bed. As soon as she stepped out of the kitchen, the ugly mirror appeared in her peripheral, her hands trembling with the urge to destroy it, and she couldn't keep it down. A guttural roar tore from her chest as she rushed toward it. She debated between flinging it across the room or punching right through.

Before she could decide, a flash of something on the reflective surface caught her attention. She expected to see her reflection when she realized it was *Clayton's.* Eyes wide, she grabbed onto the red scales of the dragon frame, bringing her face close to the polished surface.

"Clayton?" she whispered.

The image vanished, and she was left staring at herself.

I'm imagining things, she thought and let go, taking a tentative step backward.

KAYLA FREDERICK

6.

THE INCIDENT INSTILLED something in Olivia. As a therapist, she believed strongly in talking through grief but didn't have anyone she felt she could open up to. Instead of letting it out, she took a couple sleeping pills and spent the rest of her day in a state of blissful unconsciousness. In the days to come, she would confront her grief, but today was not the day.

"Olivia! Olivia!" Clayton's voice called.

In her half-asleep daze, she called, "What?" before she remembered what had happened. Clayton was gone—*dead*. She couldn't really be hearing his voice.

It was a dream.

She choked back a sob and turned over, settling back into the blankets. If she could, she wanted it to resume, to go back to a place where Clayton was still alive.

As soon as she began to drift away, tapping drifted into her room from the hall. It sounded lighter than footsteps but more consistent than the house settling.

I'm hearing things.

She pulled the blanket up over her face and thought about everyone they'd left behind when they moved. Her phone said it was two in the morning, but she had the sudden desire to call one of her friends. To tell them everything that had happened since they'd arrived.

Maybe then, she'd stop hearing and seeing things that weren't there. *You're suppressing your grief so your brain is trying to force you into facing it anyway it can,* she would've told a patient if they had come into her office, describing her exact situation. She would've told them to not be afraid of their feelings. To embrace it. To remember their lost loved one with warmth.

Olivia tried to do that. To some extent, she succeeded, but ultimately, it was all clouded over with confusion from that last night of Clayton's life. Those few hours where Clayton *wasn't* Clayton. The red ring of fingerprints that had darkened to bruises.

They were all that remained of him now.

"Olivia!" his voice came to her again, soft and lilting, almost as if he were calling her to pull her into a gentle embrace.

She bolted upright in bed. Hearing his voice before could be written off as a dream. But she was wide awake now.

"Olivia! Help me!" The gentle voice turned to terror, desperation. *Pain.*

Olivia squeezed her eyes shut, pretending she couldn't hear it. *My job is to fix these kinds of things,* she thought, reaching up to clamp her hands over her ears. *But who can fix me?*

Clayton called out again, and no matter how hard she tried to block it out, she could still hear him. For added effect, she put her pillow over her head, but his voice came through as clearly as if he were speaking directly into her ear.

"Help me!" he cried again.

His terror won over any logic she could've used.

Feet padding down the hall, she found herself approaching the mirror. Her mind went hazy, and when she came back to herself, she was staring into it, hands clutched to the dragon scales to pull herself close.

Clayton's reflection looked back.

He whimpered, eyes giant in the magnified glass. "Olivia!

Oh, God! Please help me!"

Olivia could only stare. He looked so real, so *clear*, that it brought tears to her eyes. There was no way she was imagining this. No way she *could*.

"Clayton," she whispered.

He held his hand to the glass, fingertips pressing against the surface. Without thinking, she pressed her hand to his, and when she opened her eyes, Clayton was beside her. The air around them was black, but she hardly stopped to wonder where she was. To wonder where *they* were. She pulled him into a hug.

Then reality reared its ugly head.

Clayton was *dead*. She had seen his body. Or what was left of it anyway.

He didn't hug her back, and she pulled away. There were tears in his eyes. He certainly didn't look *happy*.

"It got you too," a voice whispered from the shadows.

She jumped, not expecting there to be anyone else with them. A figure shambled toward them, and she recognized him. Not that she'd ever met him. But she'd seen his picture. It was the man who had lived in their house before them. The missing resident.

"What are you—" she started to ask.

She turned around and looked into her own eyes.

Taking a step back, Olivia tried to understand what she was seeing. Through a thin, gray surface, her clone waved, an eerie grin spreading across its face before it held up a white sheet, hiding itself and the room behind it.

MEMENTO MORI

*Everyone is afraid of something.
Fear is a motivator, a guide, but in the end, we're all afraid of the same thing—death.*

KAYLA FREDERICK

MEMENTO MORI

Fear

IT WAS THE dust in my lungs that caught my attention first. I coughed, pebbles beneath me moving away in a clatter. My eyes shot open. Pulling myself to my feet, I made out the dusty stone walls on either side of me through a strange gray haze.

It didn't look familiar, and I had no idea where I was. The last thing I remember was the van, then blackness. Now I'm here.

I traced the wall to the path ahead of me. A walkway of sorts. Before I could move, the sound of a motor starting up came from nearby, rumbling through the silence like a horde of bumblebees. A speaker lowered from the sky, hovering before me.

"Good morning," it said politely. "This is a maze. You have one hour to reach the center. Beware of wrong turns, and good luck."

As the speaker buzzed away, there was faint cheering and clapping, but I couldn't see anyone else. A loud beep came from my wrist where a heavy silver watch had been strapped in place.

The screen displayed sixty minutes.

I stared at it. If whoever was responsible for this was communicating with me, it made sense that they must be watching me somehow, but I couldn't spot a camera. "What is this?" I called, to no one in particular. "What happens if I don't make it out in an hour?"

Silence. I was left alone with my questions.

Was the center of the maze the only way out?

If it was, what happened if I made a wrong turn?

I have to get out of here.

With careful steps, I ventured into the fog, running my fingers along the dusty stone wall. The path was straight for a while, and I convinced myself I could do this. I could find my way out. When I did, I would go to the police and put an end to this...whatever *this* was. Then the path split, and all my certainty washed away. I stood at the fork, peering down each path. Which one was the right choice?

What would happen if I chose wrong?

A buzz from my watch told me I had fifty-eight minutes left. There were no clues guiding me. I had to decide, alone. I chose the left corridor, and as my feet left the main hall, a large, silver door clanged shut behind me.

That's not a good sign.

Something skittered across the pebbles on the floor behind me, and I whipped around, trying to find the source. The fog was too thick to see through, so I crept onward, guard raised. A slick spot on the floor caught my attention. It was an enormous web that snaked up the wall like a Halloween decoration. Then I realized what I was looking at wasn't fog—silver strands of web coated the corridor like streamers.

"Spiders? Why does it have to be spiders?" I whispered to myself as I continued forward.

I ripped my foot free from the web and continued onward, feeling worse with every step. The pattering sounded again, and a giant shadow appeared ahead. It raced toward me, and I ducked out of the way, pressing against the wall as it passed.

The spider was the size of a small horse. Dotted with blue

and black, green slime dripped from its massive jaws.

"Help!" I cried, taking off down the hallway.

The mutated spider followed in close pursuit. I tried to pick up my pace, but I could see the end of the corridor. If I went down there, I would be trapped. Skidding to a halt, I leaned against the wall, panting. People were watching this, watching my struggle.

Would they come to rescue me?

Or did they want me to fail?

My eyes darted everywhere, searching for some way out. Beneath the webs, on the other wall, was a lattice fence. A glint at the top caught my attention. The spider blocked the end of the corridor. To get to the lattice, I would have to pass it. Swallowing roughly, I stared the spider down. It lunged, and I ducked beneath its snapping jaws, racing toward the anomaly. I leapt onto it, swathes of webs clinging to my face and arms, threatening to hold me in place.

I shook them off as the spider reached the bottom of the lattice, clicking its giant legs together in what I guessed was a preparation to grab me. I didn't look down, afraid I'd see how close it was and lose my nerve. I reached for the item—a sword tied through the top loop. Gripping the handle, I tried to pull it free, but the rope held tight.

The lattice rattled as the spider jumped on it. It landed inches from my leg, baring its fangs to sink into my skin. With another desperate yank, the sword came free, and I swung. The spider reared back, trying to bite me as it screeched and raged, casting green slime in every direction.

I let go of the lattice and fell, sword held out before me.

KAYLA FREDERICK

The metal blade sliced through the enormous arachnid, covering me in slime as I hit the ground. The spider's body landed with a *thump* beside me. Disgusted, I struggled to my feet.

The familiar buzz of the speaker sounded. "Congratulations. You have passed your first challenge. As a result, you may keep the sword."

The sound of an auditorium full of clapping filled the air as it ascended back into the sky.

The door that had sealed me in this chamber opened, allowing me to choose the other path in the fork. I wiped the disgusting mix of slime and spider webs off my face and kept going.

My watch announced forty-five minutes left.

I continued onward, feeling sick. If that was only the first challenge, what else did the maze have to offer? I stopped to lean against the wall, hoping to compose myself before I moved on. The gentle gray fog became darker, thicker, changing from smoke gray to sable black before I reached the next fork.

A quick game of eenie-meenie-miney-moe decided that I'd take the right corridor. No door shut behind me, and I continued down the walkway, hand on the wall and sword ready in case something else descended on me.

In the distance came ethereal growling, and I knew before I saw it that there would be another fork in the path. In my head, I charted the part of the labyrinth that I'd already explored. The right path had been the correct answer twice so far.

It couldn't be right again...right?

Listen for the sound, I told myself.

But the growling stopped. Heart pounding with

anticipation, I looked left and right, then at the ticking second hand on my watch. I was wasting time. Time I didn't have. With a heavy breath, I stepped into the left corridor, the metallic *clang* announcing the path shutting behind me.

"Damn it," I cursed, glaring at the door before I faced whatever lie ahead.

The floor glowed red, the color of lava. The walls were black as night, making it impossible to distinguish them from the smoke in the air. Growling echoed from the center.

Whatever it was, it was big.

A shape materialized. Two enormous canine heads, both mouths full of razor-sharp teeth on top of a beast's body. It charged, and I slashed with the sword, but the blade went right through its snout, parting like smoke before rearranging itself.

The sword slid from my fingers.

This wasn't a dog. It was a *hellhound*.

Don't look in its eyes, I thought as I ducked around it. *It'll kill you that way.*

The beast pounded after me, snapping at me with both sets of teeth. My best bet at survival was to flee. After all, how could I hurt something made of shadows? But I wouldn't be able to run forever.

On the other side of the pit, a beam of light appeared, piercing through the darkness to highlight an object on the ground.

That must be it...that must be the answer!

I bounded toward it, but a second before I grabbed it, the hound's teeth sank into the skin on my calf. Crying out, I dropped to the ground. It clamped down harder, and I couldn't feel myself hit the ground over the tearing of muscle. Tears streamed down my face, but I refused to look at my leg or at the beast mauling it. I focused on the light, inching closer to the object. I was close enough to see it now, a piece of broken glass. My fingers wrapped around it, and the second head bit my other calf.

The shard sliced the skin on my palm, but I barely noticed the new pain over the pain in my legs. I held the piece up into the light, angling it toward the Hellhound. A golden beam pierced through the thick shadows of its neck. The beast howled and released me, disappearing like mist. I lay on the ground, panting and trying to absorb what had happened.

The familiar whirring of the approaching speaker roared overhead. "Congratulations on overcoming your second challenge," it said. "The center is close. You should be proud. Not very many make it this far."

How many others had they done this to? How many of them had *survived*? I chucked the mirror shard at it. "What? No prize this time?"

It was silent as it floated away into the darkness overhead.

Life is enough.

I almost hadn't made it out with that much.

The pain in my legs was intense, and I was afraid to see the extent of the damage. Reaching toward my calf, I poked the destroyed flesh, trying to paint an image with touch alone. I wasn't prepared for the truth.

It's okay, you're okay, I told myself and tried to stand. That was a mistake. The pain was unbearable, and I relied on the wall to keep from falling again. Only thirty minutes left, and my legs were all but useless.

MEMENTO MORI

Using the wall, I hobbled back down the corridor, stopping to pick up the sword I'd discarded at the beginning of the fight. It made a good walking stick as I backtracked to the fork, mad at myself for not choosing the right path to begin with.

With each step, blood leaked down my leg and onto the ground. I wondered how much longer I'd be able to continue before my adrenaline gave out. The stones on the wall changed from dingy grey boulders to intricate white tiles with blue diamonds painted on the center. I remembered what the speaker had told me about getting closer to the end, and I felt a bit better, despite my condition.

I was almost free.

I glanced at my watch. Time was dissolving faster than the progress I made. With ten minutes left, the corridor seemed endless. My steps grew shorter and shorter, and I feared that it wouldn't be long before I collapsed.

The speaker dropped down before me, greeting me with a buzz. "You have five minutes to reach the center. You may want to consider picking up the pace or you'll face the consequences."

"I'm hurt, can't you see that?" I screamed, hoping for some sign of remorse.

It offered none. "Good luck," it said before it once again floated away.

They're hoping I die in here, I thought bleakly. Whoever was pulling the strings wanted a bloody show. They didn't want victory.

Five minutes remained on my watch, and I forced myself up, struggling to take every step. The minutes bled away until only one remained, ticking down to fifty-nine seconds. The watch screen magnified every number.

Rumbling sounded behind the walls, and I didn't want to think about what it meant. Up ahead was a bend in the walkway, and I assumed it led to the center of the maze. If I could make it there, I'd be safe. Ten feet from the end of the path, the tiles behind me began to fall away, revealing an abyss that was probably littered with skeletons—if it had an end at all. The floor fell away faster and faster until I was forced to swing forward in a kind of jump, losing the sword. I landed in the center of the maze as the tile I'd stood on disappeared.

I rested my cheek on the cold surface and let out a few tears before I propped myself on my elbows and dragged myself a little farther from the edge. "Well? I did it! I'm here! Let me out!" I shouted, voice echoing around the stone room.

The room began to swirl. I couldn't keep going, not without help.

Thump. Something moved in the wall, like a giant switch had been flipped. Then the walls inched closer. I tried to stand but couldn't summon the energy. I rolled over onto my back, staring up at the ceiling covered in spikes. The walls moved closer, shaking the entire room. My heart raced, but I didn't move—I couldn't. I should have known there was no escaping the maze alive. I could die in one of two ways: leap into the dark pit or be crushed to death.

I laughed, overcome with hysteria.

Closing my eyes, I lay still, feeling my blood pool in a sticky puddle beneath me as I waited for death to claim me.

Not much longer now.

The thump sounded again, and I opened my eyes as the

MEMENTO MORI

walls began to recede. The familiar buzz filled my ears, the speaker hovering above me like a metallic vulture.

"Congratulations. You have conquered your fears."

I smiled as black unconsciousness swept over me.

KAYLA FREDERICK

MEMENTO MORI

Is there a Heaven or a Hell? How are we so sure we aren't already in one or the other? What's paradise to some is damnation to others.

KAYLA FREDERICK

MEMENTO MORI

Happy Birthday

ANGEL TURNED OVER in bed and stared at the clock. Two minutes until midnight. Not just *any* midnight. The midnight of her birthday. A sigh escaped her lips as she thought of the wishes she was sure would litter her social media accounts in a few hours. Ignoring the urge to get up and check them, she cuddled deeper into her pillows. The phone on her nightstand lit up with a message. Angel squinted in the darkness as she reached for it.

It was an email from her college. "Happy birthday, Angel!" it read.

She clicked the phone off, settling back into her sheets. The smell of smoke made them pop open a beat before the shrill ring of the fire alarm hit her eardrums. Throwing the blanket off, she ran down the hallway, following a smoke trail.

She rounded the corner and into the kitchen. Flames devoured her stovetop. With a gasp, she rushed to the stove and flipped the knob off. Without fuel, the flames sparked, licking at the curtains framing the window above the sink. Angel filled a pan with water and dumped it on the stove, extinguishing the blaze before it could get out of control. Heart pounding, she ran her fingers through her hair and dropped the pan with a clang on the counter. A burnt piece of curtain fluttered to the ground.

Four, a voice whispered.

Feeling hot breath in her ear, she wheeled around, worried

that whoever had set the fire had found her, but she was alone.

It can't be, she thought, licking her dry lips.

Angel cast another wary glance to her stove before becoming aware of the ugly noise of the fire alarm. Stepping back into the hall, she noticed the low battery indicator flashing before it went out with an eerie, clipped squeal.

That must be what I heard earlier, she reasoned. Slinking back to her room, she returned to bed with an uneasy weight on her shoulders.

***

SLEEP WAS HARD to come by that night. From the few winks she managed to get, Angel awoke in cold sweat, her heart beating so hard it hurt.

The nightmare came back to her, a memory from a year prior.

Mia. Angel's faithful companion for a decade. The calico cat had seen Angel through the best times of her life. When she grew old, it was Angel's turn to take care of her. Angel didn't know how the feisty feline had slipped from the apartment, but when she saw she was gone, she went to search for her. Mia was on the other side of the road when she found her. Angel hurried across, desperate to catch her friend before something bad happened to her.

One moment, she was on her feet. The next? She lay on the ground. She never saw the car that hit her, but she felt the point of impact in her hip where it shattered. Pain overwhelmed her, and she didn't hear the woman crouched beside her, waving her hands above Angel's broken body, clueless how to help. Her gaze focused on the sky as her peripheral vision blackened. Someone called nine-one-one, but she knew it was too late.

Death was coming to claim her.

Her vision shrunk to the size of a pinhead, as if she were falling down a well, before disappearing completely—her pain along with it. When she opened her eyes again, she felt an odd sense of freedom. The burden of her consciousness had been lifted. The tiny room she found herself in was mostly covered in shadows except for one spotlight illuminating a figure dressed in black.

He sat in a padded red chair, watching her approach through steely gray eyes. "Greetings and salutations."

"W-what's going on?" Angel whispered, finding it impossible to break eye contact.

He leaned forward, elbows resting on his knees, and said, "I'm here to make you a deal."

"A-a deal?" she stuttered then froze with realization. "Y-you're the devil! What could you possibly have to offer me?"

"I prefer to be called *Lucifer*," he stated, a hint of a smirk on his thin lips.

She waited for him to continue, not liking what that look said.

"You can have your life back, *but* you must bring me a soul in exchange."

"You mean, *kill* someone?" she said, almost outraged that he would ask. She wasn't a killer. "I can't do that. You might as well take my soul now."

"Don't be so hasty," he said as if he hadn't heard her. "On

your next birthday you will be given five chances. For each time your birthday is acknowledged, you will lose a piece of your soul. If you give me a life before your soul is gone, I will return the pieces, and you will be off the hook, scot-free. If the day passes, and you still have pieces, but haven't brought me a soul, I'll let you slide until the year after that."

"What if I can't do it?" she peeped, watching him rise to his feet. He smirked, stalking toward her in an almost sensual manner as he brought his face close. "Then you die."

That had been a year ago. Enough time for her injuries to have healed, and Mia to pass away from old age, but that nightmare she'd had during her surgery still regularly came back, unsettling her every time.

Angel hopped up out of bed and took a shower to clear her mind, dressing before looking at her rugged appearance in the mirror.

Concealer can't help me today.

Leaving the apartment, she locked the door behind her and lugged her heavy handbag onto her shoulder.

The doorman glanced up at her as she stepped into the lobby. "Good morning, Angel."

She nodded weakly, leaning against his desk. She regretted not getting a cup of coffee before leaving her apartment.

He cocked an eyebrow. "You didn't sleep well, I take it?"

She shook her head, pursing her lips. "I-uh—I may have had a brief firefighting episode last night, Gerard," she said, thinking it to be the easiest way to explain what happened.

"Not too bad, I hope," Gerard replied, eyeing her in concern.

MEMENTO MORI

"Nothing I couldn't handle," Angel said and glanced at her watch. "Hey, I'm running kind of late. I'll talk to you later."

"Okay, well, in case I don't see you again today, happy birthday!" he called after her as she walked out the door.

She pretended not to hear. The words made her soul *very* uncomfortable for a reason she couldn't place. She resumed her journey to the bus stop, worried she'd miss it. The last thing she needed was to be late again. Determined to put away the night's incident as nothing more than an accident, Angel crossed the street and headed into the less-than-reputable part of town.

Then she heard it—a snarl.

It's my imagination, she thought, picking up the pace.

She slipped her hand into the pocket where she kept a can of pepper spray. A rough bark sounded behind her, and she stole a glance over her shoulder. Nothing but shadows from the nearby trees.

See? It's nothing, she tried to convince herself, as she scanned the empty space.

When she looked over her shoulder this time, she noticed a thicker patch of black shadows in the middle of the rest. It shifted, moving closer before it materialized into a dog the size of a small horse with ruby red eyes. It pulled its lips back into a snarl, showing its sharp, dagger-like teeth. She tried to run, the only thing her body could think to do, but didn't make it far down the nearest alley before the beast appeared in front of her again, an angry, dark shadow of burning hatred.

It charged. Although the beast had come from thin air, it weighed a ton when it tackled her to the ground, sending the pepper spray flying into the grass. She shoved it but was unable to push the massive hound off her chest before it ripped a chunk of flesh from her arm.

She cried out and tried to strike it, but her punches went through it. She squeezed her eyes shut as the teeth dipped closer to her throat. Before they sank into her flesh, the beast's weight disappeared, and the voice whispered in her ear again.

Three.

Her eyes opened, darting everywhere to search the alley for whoever had helped her. But again, she was alone. Her arm had been mutilated, chunks of muscle hanging outside of her skin to reveal a hint of her paper white bone beneath. A wave of nausea climbed up her chest, and she forced it down, holding her arm close to her as she whimpered and struggled to her feet.

Dizziness surged through her, and she used the brick wall to keep steady. She made it to the end of the alley, leaning against the wall to stay conscious. Blood poured to the ground, and a woman coming down the street stopped to stare at her.

"Oh, my God," she gasped, hand covering her mouth. "What happened?"

"P-please…call nine-one-one…I-I'm very hurt," Angel rasped, struggling to hold what was left of the meat on her arm.

Angel's vision wavered as the woman made the call, and she slumped to the ground, praying she would not pass out. She was afraid of what waited for her in the dark. The woman sat beside her, a hand on her shoulder. She stayed with Angel until the ambulance arrived, whispering comforting words. At least, Angel *assumed* they were comforting. She didn't hear most of them because her mind was elsewhere—on the eyes of the beast so similar in color to the blood leaking from her arm.

MEMENTO MORI

Caught up in her delusion, she didn't notice the emergency workers surrounding her. She blipped out of consciousness, and when she came to, the woman was gone, replaced by a man named Tom, sitting beside her in the back of the emergency vehicle. She was strapped to a table but had no memory of being placed on it. Her wallet was in his hand, and he glanced at her driver's license.

"Your name is Angel?" he asked. From his tone, she guessed he'd already asked a handful of times, with no response.

Angel managed a small nod.

"Well, not a very happy birthday for you, huh?" he said, a small chuckle escaping his lips as he tucked the card back in place.

No, she whispered. Closing her eyes, she succumbed to the blood loss.

***

WHEN SHE REGAINED consciousness, Angel couldn't move. She might have thought she were dead had it not been for the blinding pain in her arm. She tried to swallow, but her throat was so dry, she nearly choked. Tears bubbled up in her eyes from the hitch in her breathing. When it cleared, it was replaced by a continuous beeping sound. Only, she couldn't move her head to figure out what it was.

What's happening?

"Hand me the scalpel."

The voice cut through the rhythmic beeping, and the odor of sterilized cleaners filled Angel's nose. She felt a twinge of pain in her heart as she realized she was in the hospital. They were about to perform surgery on her arm. She tried to open her eyes, but they wouldn't budge. She couldn't speak either.

A silent scream rang out in her mind, then she felt it—the scalpel cutting away pieces of muscle from her devastated flesh. Wave after wave of pain rushed through her, like a kind of medieval torture. She tried to wiggle her fingers, to twitch any muscle to gain their attention, but nothing happened.

The pain continued, and she wished, nearly *prayed*, for death as she lay on the operating table in her own personalized Hell.

Two, the voice floated through her mind, taking her to blackness when it faded.

***

ANGEL WOKE in a white room so bright it blinded her. Like before, the pain brought her back to life, so she knew she was still alive. This time, she could move, much to her relief. Glancing around, she saw she was in a cubicle in the emergency room, her damaged arm covered in soft white cloths. What exactly had the surgery done for her? She traced the IV line beside her to the bag of saline solution above her bed. Smacking her dry lips, she longed for a cup of water. The idea of human interaction prevented her from pressing the call button.

Tik-tok, a voice whispered in her ear.

A sickening feeling washed over her. It was real—the meeting with the devil, the warning, the *voice*. That nightmare hadn't been a nightmare after all. That meant three of her chances were already gone, and her birthday was only half-over.

MEMENTO MORI

I can't kill anyone.

That thought brought a chuckle to the back of her mind. She knew it was his.

I need to get out of here, she decided. She needed to find a place to go, somewhere *safe*, until her nightmare was over. Ripping the IV from her arm, she wrapped the bed sheet around the wound and hurried to get dressed.

She peeked out into the hall and dashed from the room, cradling her mauled arm to her chest. Everyone stared as she shouldered past nurses, running through the halls, into the lobby, and out the front door. Shouts sounded behind her, but she didn't stop—it was too risky. She ran all the way back to her apartment, ignoring Gerard on her way through the lobby, and bolted up the stairs.

In her apartment, she went straight to her bed, pulling her knees up to her chest before the tears came. How had her life come to this?

I'm glad I didn't check Facebook today. Angel scoffed. She still had two pieces left, and she had to make them count.

The phone in her pocket rang. Her mother was calling.

Voicemail. If it's important, she'll leave a voicemail.

Less than twenty seconds later, her phone lit up with a voicemail. Angel felt that sickening feeling in the pit of her stomach again. The decision should have been easy—ignore the voicemail until tomorrow.

But what if it was an emergency?

Her desire to know outweighed her fear, and she picked the phone up. Entering the passcode, she held the phone to her ear. "Hey, Angel. Since you never answer your phone, I wanted to tell you happy birth—"

Angel rushed to hang up, but it wasn't fast enough. She heard it.

"No! No...no..." she whimpered, searching for anything that could bring her harm. She didn't hear the cracking of the chain that held the shelf above her bed until it was too late. The heavy snow globe fell, striking her in the back of the skull before it shattered, embedding glass in the skin on her neck and shoulders. Angel moaned but managed to stay conscious as she crawled forward, getting out of range before anything else could strike her.

One, the voice echoed in her head.

Angel's heart pounded as she struggled to stay on her feet. Across her apartment, someone knocked on the front door. Angel struggled to lift her head, to see out in the hallway.

Hell of a time for a guest.

Then a worse sound—her door opened.

"Angel! My God! Are you in here?" said Miranda, her friend and neighbor.

I must've screamed, Angel realized in heart-wrenching defeat, her hand clutching the bed post to try to prop herself up.

"I-I'm fine, just an accident," Angel called, doing her best to get off the bed in what she hoped was a normal-looking manner so Miranda would *leave*.

Miranda did the opposite. She appeared in the doorframe, rushing to her side. "You need to go to the hospital," she said, wiping the glass off Angel's shoulders and poking the glass stuck in the back of her neck. "This is bad!"

"Please go home," Angel said, feeling her mouth run dry

again.

"I'm not gonna leave you alone in this condition on your birthday of all days."

Angel's mouth fell open as she stared at her friend. Thick tears formed in the corners of her eyes.

She was out of time.

"Angel? Angel, what's wrong?" Miranda demanded, grabbing Angel's arms to try to make her friend meet her eyes.

"I love you, Miranda, don't ever change," she choked, letting her eyes meet Miranda's for the last time.

From the corner of her eye, she saw him standing in the entrance to her bedroom, knife in his hand.

"I'm here to collect on my debt, darling," he said, eyes shining as he crept toward her.

"No…no!" Angel shrieked, pulling herself from her friend's grasp. She fell backward onto the bed, glass shards prickling her skin.

"What? What is it?" Miranda demanded, her gaze darting around, but unable to see the literal demon in the room.

Lucifer stepped up to Angel, grasping her jaw in his free hand as the first of her tears leaked free.

"Deep down, you knew it would come to this," he whispered.

He pressed his lips to hers and plunged the knife through her heart. She grabbed her chest and collapsed. What sounded like miles away, Miranda wailed, utterly confused by her friend's fate.

Lucifer's passing words swam in Angel's mind as she lay dying in a pool of her own blood.

Never make a deal with the devil unless you're prepared to lose.

KAYLA FREDERICK

About the Author

A little neurotic and a huge lover of Halloween, Kayla enjoys creepy stories and cats.